Helen's response was cut short by a loud crash from just outside the building. Without thinking Helen grabbed Cecily by the arms and moved protectively in front of her. One hand groped to her side in search of a gun that wasn't there — a hangover from her old days as a cop. With a muttered curse, Helen forced herself to stay still as she listened intently. The room darkened as a cloud passed over the sun, filtering out what light had reached into the room.

Footsteps crunched on broken glass and rock outside. "What the hell is going on? You're hurting my arm," Cecily gasped into Helen's ear.

Helen felt her skin tingle as Cecily's warm breath moved over her neck. She was sharply aware of the girl's slender softness as she yielded to Helen's firm grasp. "Sorry," Helen mumbled, loosening her fingers. Cecily moved closer. Her chest rose and fell perceptibly, brushing Helen's back. "Someone is moving around out there . . ."

About the Author

Pat Welch was born in Japan in 1957. When her family returned to the United States she grew up in the South until settling in California in 1976. She has lived and worked in the San Francisco Bay area since 1986. *A Proper Burial* is the third novel in the Helen Black mystery series.

A Proper Burial

A Helen Black Mystery by
Pat Welch

The Naiad Press, Inc.
1993

Printed in the United States of America on acid-free paper
First Edition

Edited by Christine Cassidy
Cover design by Pat Tong and Bonnie Liss
   (Phoenix Graphics)
Typeset by Sandi Stancil

Library of Congress Cataloging-in-Publication Data

Welch, Pat, 1957–
   A proper burial : a Helen Black mystery / by Pat Welch.
      p.   cm.
   ISBN 1-56280-033-7 : $9.95
   1. Lesbians—Fiction.   I. Title.
PS3573.E4543P76   1993
813'.54—dc20   92-41947
                                                            CIP

To my sisters

Chapter One

Jeremy and Hallie looked at Martin Pfister with anger. "So where is it?" Jeremy demanded, leaning his huge frame over the smaller boy.

Martin smelled the leather of Jeremy's black jacket, the stale cigarette stench that always accompanied him. Behind him, Hallie tossed her long blonde hair and narrowed her green eyes. Martin's fear of Jeremy melted in the heat of his lust for Hallie.

"You said there was a big stash here, right?" Jeremy said. "In the old building."

"That's right. I'm sure of it. I see these guys going in and out of here all the time," Martin sputtered, shoving his glasses up more securely on his nose. "I know they're hiding stuff away in here." His voice broke and he winced to see Hallie laughing.

"Come on, Jeremy, this is a fucking waste," she said, twisting her slim body in its skin-tight black sheath as she climbed over a pile of rubble to join them. "Let's get the hell out of here. It gives me the creeps."

"Yeah, me too." Jeremy nodded as they all stood and surveyed the ugly scene. The Darcy Building, adjoining an abandoned lot that had been taken over by the homeless pushed out of People's Park, loomed like something out of a war zone. It had a history of bad luck — first the earthquake of 1989 had exposed its unsafe condition, then the 1991 fire finished the job.

The roof was caving in throughout the once-elegant apartment building. Walls gaped to the outside world, revealing broken beams and crumbled brickwork. The Condemned signs slapped across entrances and windows had done little to discourage people from coming and going — most of the signs had been torn off and flung haphazardly onto the scattered debris surrounding the front entrance.

Jeremy and Hallie turned back to Martin. "All right, asshole, where? Huh?" Jeremy pushed Martin's thin frame with one meaty hand. Hallie folded her arms and waited.

Martin swallowed hard. "I saw them going through the front. Right there. They were carrying these bags."

2

"A bunch of homeless fags, probably. What makes you think it was more than just the shit they find in the streets?"

Hallie looked at the building, then at Jeremy. "Why the hell not? We could at least take a look, huh?"

"Right! That's why I brought you guys here," Martin said, warming to her interest. "Hey, I even got a flashlight in the Spider — why don't I go get it?" He was scrambling away from Jeremy as he spoke, but not in time to avoid hearing his response.

"That's right. The big Boy Scout gonna get his big flashlight."

Martin walked more quickly to the red sports car so he didn't have to hear Hallie laughing at Jeremy's stab at humor. He knew that the shiny car — the freedom from parental restraint that it promised, the hint of wildness it gave to his all-too-ordinary appearance — was the only reason people like Jeremy and Hallie would condescend to spend two minutes in his presence.

The car was parked around the corner on Dwight Way, in front of a dingy student apartment building. Its small size had allowed Martin to squeeze the vehicle in front of a service van next to a huge tree, with only a tip of the back fender poking out into the street. Martin had a fleeting memory of the way Hallie's tight, slim thighs had slid over his legs when she got out of the car not half an hour ago, laughingly escaping from her perch next to the gearshift. Jeremy's big hand had appreciatively patted her bottom as she passed over Martin's lap, and Martin had had to remain in the car for a moment, forcing himself to control his groin's automatic response to her rounded behind.

3

The sweet memory faded when he saw his reflection in the car window. It was the same old face — thin, pale, pimply, made more ridiculous by the thick glasses he'd had to wear all his life, the nose sticking out like a fake bit of plastic some joker had glued on. Flashlight in hand, he grimly slammed the door and went back down Dwight.

He had to scurry past two men on the sidewalk, one pushing a shopping cart filled with unnameable piles of stuff, the other wearing at least three coats in the warm spring air. Both men smelled of whiskey, sweat and urine. Martin found them terrifying, but he cast his eyes toward the sidewalk and butted through. They stood, unmoving, refusing to get out of his way. In fact they seemed to find him amusing. "You better get back to your friends," one of them growled. "They up there in the Darcy."

Martin looked up. He'd had no idea they were being observed. He started to back away, then the other one said, "Maybe the ghost got 'em."

Martin tried to laugh, but it came out as a high-pitched wheeze. "You're — you're full of shit, you know that?" As he spoke, his thoughts were filled with fear for Hallie. Was there someone hiding in the building, waiting for her? Martin glanced down at the hands of the man who had spoken. Was there another pair of hands like these even now stripping her clothes off, rubbing the contours of her body with pleasure, sliming her with grime and filth?

"You don't believe in ghosts, do ya?" The two men advanced on him. The shopping cart squeaked as it bumped over the sidewalk. Everything else seemed to have gone quite still, and Martin froze

4

before them. "Well, you ought to spend some time with us in People's Park. They's lots of ghosts there. I see 'em all the time." The first man grinned as he delivered this statement, and Martin felt an impulse to giggle at the gap created by the missing teeth in his dark gums. The other man snickered, then began to pick his nose.

Martin tried to shut out their laughter as he ran back to the Darcy Building. He was relieved to see its weird Gothic ruin looming up before him as he rounded the corner. A quick backward glance assured him that he wasn't being followed by the two men, and the area around the building was deserted. As calmness took over, he was ashamed of the fact he was sweating. A few deep breaths later, he switched on the flashlight and crouched just inside the jagged entrance to the Darcy Building.

"Hallie? Jeremy? It's me, Martin," he whispered into the darkness. The tiny circle of light danced over the opposite wall, showing neither color nor object nor shape to disturb the dead, flat surface. A few shafts of light, given entrance by holes in the walls and ceiling, had an odd beauty as they descended into the void. Once his eyes had grown accustomed to the murky blackness, Martin relaxed a little more. No furniture remained in what had been the Darcy's lobby. But wood and brick and uneven clumps of fallen concrete reminded him of the danger he and his friends faced the longer they stayed here. "Hallie? Jeremy? Where are you? Come on, you guys!" He no longer whispered, but still there was no response.

Slowly Martin picked his way through the room. A trickle of dirt and plaster sifted under the collar of his shirt, and in a panic he brushed it away. It was then that he heard them. Going farther and farther into the room, he followed the sound, not sure if it was a ghost or his friends. The slow rhythm of their moans, the unmistakable gentle thud repeating itself, the rustle of fabric sliding on flesh — Martin knew what he would see before he saw it. He turned a corner and there they were. Jeremy's body moved like a piston between Hallie's outstretched legs, while she clutched at his buttocks with tightening fingers. They turned to look at Martin, then closed their eyes again as they neared climax.

Torn between disgust and desire and anger, Martin backed away, dropping the flashlight as he went back to the main room. They could do that — in a place like this, full of death and destruction — and they didn't even care if he saw them! "Fuck you," he muttered, punching one weak, tentative fist against a wall. Then his voice grew stronger, born of years of frustration and hurt, years of never belonging, no matter how hard he tried, all the times he had just wanted a friend. "Fuck you!" he shouted, as much to cover their cries of pleasure as to vent his rage. The fist shot out again, with enormous force this time. Martin put his hand right through the wall before he knew what he'd done. It crashed a hole that caused him to fall forward, pushing his arm into the other side up to his elbow. Terrified, Martin nearly screamed. Then, as he started wiggling his hand around, he felt weak with joy. It didn't seem to be broken. But how to get it out? Martin gently turned his arm this way and that, but the hole seemed to be closing in on him.

6

Screwing up his eyes and his courage, Martin gave one huge yank, nearly convinced he would lose the limb in the process.

To his amazement, the arm emerged whole and sound. The wall wasn't so lucky, however. Cheap fiberboard splintered and fell off the wall, then the whole surface groaned. Martin stared, feeling both guilty and surprised, as the wall folded in on itself and collapsed in a whispering protest of dust.

He coughed, sputtered, took off his glasses to clean them of the fine powder the dust raised. Once he had his breath and his vision again, he stepped gingerly through the hole he'd created. Even the final grunts of Jeremy and Hallie were forgotten as he peered into his discovery.

It was some sort of closet or storage space — far too small to be anything else, really. A broken broom handle and a forlorn mophead, lying in the dirt like a lonely white tarantula, seemed to justify his assumption. There was a huge mound of rags in the corner, most likely for cleaning. Martin picked up the broom handle and began to poke around. First he shoved it around the wall where he'd made his grand entrance, widening the gap. Then he turned his attention to the wall opposite, where light came in from the outside world through a series of jagged holes. One good thrust resulted in an opening that matched in size the one caused by his arm.

Standing back to view his handiwork, Martin stumbled over the rag mountain. A strange, faint odor emerged from the motion of the cloth. With distaste Martin remembered the two guys on the sidewalk. Maybe they went to the bathroom here, or something. Curiosity overcame his disgust, and he poked at the rags with the broom handle.

Martin saw the hand first. It struck with a flaccid splat against the broom handle, almost as if it were about to take it away from Martin. He screamed, grabbing his tool and clutching it with both hands. The sudden motion of the handle disarranged the rags, pulling them away to reveal what lay underneath. The knife remained lodged in the center of the thing's back, giving itself away with only a thin metallic gleam. The blank eyes, slightly sunken, stared into nothing. The face was puffy, bloated, its features blotched. Martin screamed again, and he didn't stop until after Jeremy and Hallie came running to see what the little twerp was fucking up this time.

Chapter Two

Helen looked past the head of her visitor to the frosted glass door marked "Private." She could see that the painted black lettering was chipping away from the "Helen Black" that had once looked so glossy and professional when she'd opened for business just two and a half years ago. The line underneath her name that read "Private Investigator" was in even worse shape. Maybe it was just the presence of another person in the room, but everything seemed just a bit shabbier this afternoon. The carpet showed its stains worse than before, and the droopy fern in the corner cried out for attention. Even the windows, looking out over Shattuck Avenue in downtown Berkeley, filtered the warm sunlight through streaks of greasy dirt.

Helen turned back to her ex-lover — or was that the right word? Even now she wasn't sure. Frieda had left her a year ago. "I can't stay with you until I'm more sure of myself," Frieda had said when she'd moved out. "I need some time. Don't worry — it's just an experiment."

So Helen, silent, had watched her walk away. She hadn't known how to say the words that would stop her, that would express how it hurt to see her leave. Since that terrible day they'd met twice for lunch. Both encounters had been calm and cordial, in the safety of public places. Both had left Helen feeling limp.

Then, last night, Sunday, the phone call had broken into the blare of the television set. "I think I have a new client for you, Helen," Frieda had said with careful brightness. "When can she see you?"

Now Helen looked up at Frieda and the new client, seated across the desk from her in the upholstered chairs that were just beginning to show signs of wear. Cecily Bennett stared back at her with a cool gaze from wide green eyes set over high cheekbones in a pale face framed by thick red hair swept back in a braid. Chiseled features were saved from being sharp by their small size. A thin, long-fingered hand rested motionless on the arm of the chair while the other hand reached toward Frieda, then stopped in midair. It was at that moment, in that gesture, that Helen realized Cecily and Frieda were sleeping together.

Helen glanced at Frieda just in time to see Frieda turn away from her look, slightly embarrassed. Helen noted the same paint-stained clothing and faint streaks on the face and hands, the complete lack of adornment or makeup — the same Frieda Lawrence she'd known and loved, who was always found in the torn jeans and loose T-shirt fresh from the studio where she worked. But the new haircut, sleek and smooth, pulled away from the face, resembled Cecily's style.

Helen looked down at her desk and cleared her throat to gain a moment of control. Her hands found the newspaper that Cecily had brought with her. It was an issue of the *Berkeley Herald*, dated last Thursday. Again she glanced through the article Cecily had circled. It told of the discovery Wednesday afternoon of a woman's body in the old Darcy Building, not far from the university. Apparently in her early thirties, the woman had been stabbed in the back — one fatal blow. A group of teenagers had stumbled upon the body. Medical examiners believed she had been dead less than twenty-four hours. Brief and detached, the article rounded off its few sentences with a statement that no identity had been established.

"Okay, I've read it. Fill me in," Helen said in her best hard-boiled manner as she reached for a pen and a steno pad.

"I know who the woman is. Was." Cecily's voice was cool and clear.

Helen's pen was arrested above the paper. "Have you contacted the police?" she asked, incredulous.

Cecily shook her tidy head with impatience. "No, no, you don't understand. The police identified her.

11

The woman was my aunt, Elizabeth Bennett. Aunt Liz."

Helen stared at Cecily, looking closely for signs of emotion. "I don't recall seeing anything about this in the newspapers."

"You won't. The press haven't got hold of it, and they won't for some time. If and when they do, it will be sneaked onto some back page somewhere," Cecily said, the cool surface cracking just a little to reveal sarcasm. "The family hasn't even given her a proper burial, let alone made the information public."

Helen nodded. "And why is that?"

Cecily shrugged. "Shame, I guess. Along with the launching of Project Nightlight."

Helen let the pen drop with a quiet click onto the desk. "You've lost me."

Cecily turned her green eyes to Frieda. "You didn't tell her?"

"No, not yet. Helen, Cecily is Robert Bennett's daughter."

In spite of her determination to be as reserved as possible, Helen couldn't help raising her eyebrows. "Not Bob Bennett, the governor's right-hand man?"

Cecily sighed. "One and the same, I'm afraid. I don't know why Frieda didn't tell you last night when she called."

Helen and Frieda glanced at each other, and a ghost of a familiar smile played over Frieda's face. "Probably," Helen said, "because she remembers how I feel about politicians. But never mind that now. When did the police tell you they'd identified her?" Helen picked up her pen again and began writing as Cecily spoke.

"They called Daddy on Friday night, just two days after the body had been discovered. Aunt Liz had some sort of record. Nothing big — just arrests at demonstrations during the sixties, things like that. I guess they had some kind of file on her in the computer."

Helen smiled, thinking that during her days as a cop she might very well have helped to put Aunt Liz behind bars a time or two. The smile faded when Cecily's green eyes turned trustingly to Frieda, and Helen fixed her gaze firmly on her notepad. "Why hasn't the news been released? This Project Nightlight?" she asked, a bit too sharply.

Cecily nodded. Suddenly she closed her eyes and passed one thin pale hand over her forehead, and the carefully composed exterior fractured again as a young and emotional woman leaned back in the chair with a heavy sigh. Frieda got up from her chair and stood behind Cecily, putting her hands on the girl's shoulders. Torn between pity and anger, Helen looked down at her notebook and waited for the moment to pass.

Finally Cecily spoke. "Sorry. I — I'm still not used to Aunt Liz being gone. And to die like that."

"It's okay." This kid was too cool, the brief burst of feeling contrived. Helen refused to look at Frieda, certain that her ex would pick up on the doubt she, Helen, was having about Cecily. Was this girl close to the dead woman or not? If not, why the hell was she here? "Tell me about this project."

"My father's latest brainstorm. A new committee formed by the governor to tackle problems of child abuse statewide. They hope to have shelters for kids, schools, medical attention. Not to mention prosecution for the parent or parents or adult involved."

"What does that have to do with your Aunt Liz?"

Cecily shrugged, smiled wearily. "You obviously haven't been around politicians much. Any hint of scandal, of murder and mayhem, would create a delicate situation right now. The governor is still working on getting public support and funding for the project."

"Not to mention the election coming up next year." Helen frowned, tapped her pen. The mixed emotions that had besieged her upon seeing Frieda and Cecily together in her office were, for the moment, swallowed up in curiosity. "Ms. Bennett, I'm not entirely sure what it is you'd like me to do. If this article is correct, your aunt was killed by transients from People's Park near the Darcy Building. If that's the case, the police stand a much better chance of locating her killers than I do. If that isn't the case, they would still do a better job. Whether or not the story ever makes it to the media."

Cecily, looking young and vulnerable, turned to Frieda questioningly, then back to Helen. "I'm not so sure they're going to investigate."

"What do you mean?"

"Show her, Frieda."

Puzzled, Helen watched Frieda reach for the huge shoulder bag she'd shoved under her chair. A moment or two of scrabbling in its interior resulted in the emergence of a worn envelope.

"I asked Frieda to keep this for me," Cecily said. "I didn't want anyone at home to find it."

14

Helen took a few moments to examine the envelope. It had been airmailed and looked much the worse for its travels — grimy, stained with varying colors, redolent of odd odors. She peered at the postmark. "New Delhi," she said. "She was writing from India?"

"That's definitely her handwriting," Cecily said. "And it's addressed to me."

"No return address." With careful fingers Helen removed a slip of paper from the envelope. A few words were scrawled on it. " 'Cecily, please meet me at the Shattuck Hotel on Tuesday the fifteenth. We have to talk right away. Liz.' " Helen read slowly, then looked up. "That's the day before she was discovered. What did she want to talk to you about?"

Cecily shook her head. "I — uh — I never went to the hotel. I figured I'd call or something, to let her know I wasn't coming." The girl blushed under Helen's stare.

"No one heard from her for years, then she suddenly decides she has to talk to you?" And then you can't be bothered to keep the appointment, Helen added to herself. Her disgust with Cecily Bennett was growing exponentially by the second. "What did the police say about this letter?"

"I never showed them," Cecily mumbled.

"I find that hard to believe."

Cecily snorted. "You wouldn't if you knew the governor. I'm sure he told them to leave us alone."

Helen leaned back in her chair. "Tell me, honestly, why you want to pursue this. You say yourself you never knew her."

The little girl broke through the reserved face again. Her lower lip pouted as she burst out, "All right, I know I should have talked to her. But I didn't. And now I want to find out what happened to her."

Acting again, Helen thought, as she watched Cecily's eyes move back to Frieda. What the hell was going on here?

Her lip quivered, and Helen knew that tears were very close to the surface, even if they were false. Frieda made a protective move toward her, her face woven with sympathy and affection.

Helen said, "I'm not sure I should get involved. I can't imagine that the police wouldn't be able to find out a lot more than I would. There's almost nothing to go on here." Then Helen saw the green eyes fill with tears, and Frieda turned a look in her direction that was a cross between anger and disappointment. Helen relented. "Why don't you let me think about it, Ms. Bennett? I can call you in the morning and we'll talk some more."

Animation came to the girl's face for the first time since she'd entered the office. "Oh, would you? That would be wonderful!"

Helen spent a few more minutes making sure that Cecily had nothing more to tell her, and Frieda murmured that she'd stop by Helen's house later that evening.

Helen closed the door behind them and went to the window. As Frieda's VW was pulling away from the curb, a burly man with an outdated long haircut and brown leather jacket slipped behind the wheel of a dingy green station wagon and pulled in behind them.

Chapter Three

Lydia Bennett's cane tapped along the long, dark corridor between her two large rooms and the kitchen. The thin sound, like the scrabbling of some weak insect, barely pierced the surface of silence that veiled the sprawling Bennett house. Every afternoon, the ivy-covered house darkened quickly, sunlight and warmth disappearing from within its walls as if submerged in a deep-freeze. Lydia pulled her cardigan closer, winced slightly at the twinge in her arthritic shoulder, and kept moving.

As she approached the kitchen, sound and light increased from behind the swinging door. Lydia moved slowly, averting her eyes from the family portrait that hung in the hallway. She didn't need to look at its yellowing black-and-white images to see the changes time had worked on her children and grandchildren — and on herself. The skinny body that grew skinnier each year, the white hair that was thinning into straggly wisps, the green eyes that were now pink-rimmed and bleary with age were all painfully familiar to her. It was the tall, regal woman in the photograph, with her upswept red hair, the Chanel suit and the proud smile, who was the stranger. Lydia sighed and pushed her way into the kitchen.

She'd realized halfway down the hall that she was walking into yet another feud, this time between Cecily and her older sister, Jane. Alice, Lydia's daughter-in-law, looked on helplessly while the children sputtered and screamed at one another.

"Oh, Lydia, honey, thank goodness! Maybe you can talk some sense into these two." Alice lifted a slender hand to her professionally shaped French twist, smoothing a blonde hair that had strayed. She leaned her graceful figure against the tiled table and gave off a general air of helpless distress. Her face, usually a flawless mask of carefully applied makeup and carefully maintained blank expression, was now creased with anxiety. "I just can't make them listen to me."

Lydia snorted with disgust. "I wondered what the hell all that ruckus was about," she said as she lowered herself into one of the uncomfortable kitchen chairs and hooked her cane over the table. "It woke me up and got me out of the dungeon to see what was going on."

"Oh, Lydia, honey, I wish you wouldn't call your suite the dungeon! Robert doesn't like it," Alice cooed. "Besides, sweetie, you're the one who chose to stay there."

Lydia rolled her eyes heavenward, then turned her attention to her granddaughters. "All right, girls, what is it this time?"

Cecily plopped heavily into the chair next to Lydia's. "Nothing, Gran. It was Jane who started it, anyway."

Jane let out a brief bark of laughter. "Oh, for God's sake, quit trying to sound like the Cleavers. Shit." Jane Bennett stood by the sink and looked at her family with a sneer of disgust. She resembled her mother, but in Jane the elegant figure and studied poise translated into a desperate awkwardness. The clothing, the makeup, the hair were all a clumsy imitation of her mother that succeeded in making her look pathetic.

"Jane, please!" Alice glanced at Lydia. "Your language!"

Jane groaned and sat at the table, ignoring her mother. "You want me to tell her? Fine, I'll tell her. Little perfect Cecily here has gone out and hired a private eye. How's that for headline news?"

"So what?" Cecily shouted. "So what if I did? It's about time someone did something about Liz! You're all just sitting around with hands folded in your laps, letting the police get away with doing nothing, while Liz was rotting away in that building —"

"Cecily!" Alice gasped. "My God, how can you say that in front of your grandmother!"

"Oh, can it, Alice," Lydia muttered. "It's about time somebody stated the obvious and quit tiptoeing around me as though I were an invalid." She turned to Cecily and patted the girl's hand with her wrinkled palm. "I'm glad you did it, dear," Lydia said. "Maybe we'll get to the truth of the whole thing yet."

"Terrific." Jane slumped in her chair and folded her arms across her chest, wrinkling her expensive suit. "As if Dad didn't have enough to worry about with Project Nightlight getting off the ground." She broke her pose and leaned across the table in a gesture of appeal while Alice wrung her hands and watched the group nervously. "Don't you realize what the media will do with this if they find out? They'll say there was some kind of coverup — that's why Cecily felt she had to go to a private investigator."

"So what? There probably is!" Cecily spat. "Why else would everyone ignore me when I —" She hesitated.

"What? When you what?" Lydia pressed, putting her arm around Cecily's shoulder in encouragement.

"Nothing," Cecily muttered. "Look, this is pointless." She got up from the table with a violent movement that took Lydia by surprise, sending the old woman backwards into her chair. "I've already talked to an investigator, and I intend to see this through."

"But Cecily, honey," Alice moaned, gliding across the room, "why? Just tell me that, darling. You never even knew your aunt. She was a stranger to you. Why, after all these years, do you want to pursue this?"

"Hell, Alice, if I was in better shape I'd probably go to a private eye myself." Lydia laughed. "At least somebody cares about something in this family besides their own selfish interests." She reached up to Cecily. "I hope you picked a tall, dark and handsome detective, at least."

"Huh!" Jane snorted. "That's not exactly Cecily's style, in case you hadn't noticed." Both Alice and Lydia looked at her with blank faces, and Jane turned to her sister. "Well, little sister, I guess they haven't seen it, after all."

"Seen what, dear?" Alice asked. Across her face, confusion rapidly turned to despair. "What are you trying to say?"

Jane jerked her head in Cecily's direction. "You should hire a private investigator to follow her around some evening. See what sort of places she goes into. Who she goes with." Jane pushed away from the table and stood, upending her chair in the process. "Go on, ask her, Mom. It doesn't take a genius to figure it out."

"Jane, Cecily, I just don't understand any of this." Alice sighed tearfully with another sweep of the hand across her smooth hair. "I really think you should listen to your sister, Cecily. Let the police do their work in peace."

"Shut up and leave her alone, Alice. Don't worry, no one is going to ruffle the feathers of the Women's Republican Committee," Lydia said scornfully. "At least she had the balls to do something about my only daughter's death, while the rest of you sat around with your thumbs up your collective asses."

Alice closed her eyes, and Jane snickered. Cecily managed a stiff smile.

"Now, that's better," Lydia chirped. "One big, happy typical family, aren't we? Perfect for the press. Which brings me to the reason I emerged from my lair." She looked around expectantly.

Alice gasped. "Oh, of course! I almost forgot! The press conference."

Jane sat down again. "Good God, Mother, how could you forget? Dad and I have been working on getting his face into the media for weeks."

"Well, darling, thank goodness he has someone as capable as you helping him," Alice said as she adjusted the kitchen's television set so they could all see the screen. "I'm still not much good at politics, although I try to help all I can."

The confession was meant to be endearing, but they'd all heard it too often before. Cecily and Jane sat like two marble monuments facing the screen, while Lydia shooed Alice away. "I'm fine, for God's sake. Just go sit down so I can watch my son in peace," she snapped.

Leaning forward on her cane as she perched in the chair, Lydia forgot the tension in the room, the angry faces, the stony silence emanating from her grandchildren. Impatiently she waited for the announcers to finish their prattle and proceed to the real news — her son, standing next to the governor, for the whole state to see. A whisper of worry filtered into her thoughts, dimming her pride. What if Jane was right? What if Cecily had committed a terrible blunder, one that might compromise Robert's position? Well, never mind about that now. Lydia resolutely put doubt out of her mind and relaxed, determined to enjoy the show.

Chapter Four

At the same moment that the Bennett household was positioned in front of the television set Helen was sitting on the sofa in her living room with her set tuned to the same channel. The sound was turned down very low. Helen was going through a pile of newspapers. She'd managed to dig up her copy of the *San Francisco Chronicle* that reported the discovery of the body in the Darcy Building last week. The only item in the *Chronicle*'s account that differed from the story in the Berkeley paper was the mention of three people who'd been on the spot when Liz Bennett made her final appearance in the world. Since no names were given, Helen guessed they were minors. Too bad, she thought. It would have been helpful to talk to them.

The clink of dishes in the sink brought her out of her reverie and into the present. "Boobella!" she called to her cat. Helen was answered with an innocent little mew. "Quit pretending. I know you're climbing all over the kitchen." She glanced up at the clock over the television and realized it was high time to feed the cat. She dropped the newspapers on the floor in exasperation and headed to the kitchen through the quickly darkening house.

Helen didn't have to take inventory of the place to know that it was in desperate need of a thorough cleaning. Cups and glasses were everywhere — on bookshelves, tables, chairs. A thin film of dust softened all surfaces, and the air was stale. She'd been spending so little time at home lately. Nowadays Boobella saw her only when she was asleep. There was always too much work to do, someone to visit, plenty of paperwork waiting for her at the office. Any excuse would do to escape the pounding silence of the empty house.

From the kitchen, Helen could see the empty gaps in the bookcase just off the entrance. Frieda had kept a lot of her favorite books on those shelves. Helen stared at the vacancies and idly stroked the cat, who shrugged her hand off as she devoured the bowl of food. "Wish I was hungry too," Helen murmured. She walked slowly back to the living room.

She was just deciding to fix herself a drink when she heard Robert Bennett's name announced on the television. She hurried to the sofa in time to see the glossy-haired announcer mention Project Nightlight. A still-photo of Bennett appeared on the screen while the voice-over described a press conference that had taken place several hours ago. Helen barely had time to look for a resemblance to Cecily before the screen was switched to a live recording of the press conference.

The familiar face of California's governor loomed up behind a bristling nest of microphones. The thin nose pointed out to the cameras, as if smelling something foul — possibly a liberal. A short man, he strained his voice as much as his neck while he introduced Bennett. For a moment the air was filled with the clicks and snaps of cameras going off in simultaneous explosion. Helen turned up the sound. The governor stepped off to one side and beamed as his protege began to speak. Helen found herself paying more attention to his appearance than to his words, which were quickly exposed as the same repetitious prattle spewed by politicians everywhere.

It took only a moment to see where Cecily got her pale good looks. Her father had the same green eyes, the same sharp features. His hair was not as coppery as Cecily's, but it still gleamed red under the spotlights. When he turned in the direction of the governor, referring to his generosity and support, Helen saw a few reddish-brown locks brushed over the edge of his collar, hinting in a superficial way at renegade possibilities not usually associated with a staunch conservative. She had no doubt that the muted maverick air was one he carefully cultivated.

Some of the reporters shoving microphones at him shouted questions. Bennett smiled, nodded toward those he knew, and indicated he'd answer a few.

"How is Project Nightlight going to be funded, Dr. Bennett?"

The smile faded to seriousness. "Right now we have enough in existing revenues to get the project going and maintain it for three years. Next year we'll have a bond issue up before the citizens of California. We're also funded privately by contributions from individuals and corporations, subject, of course, to state and federal law."

"Meaning higher property taxes," Helen muttered to Boobella, who had joined her on the sofa. The cat blinked and began kneading Helen's leg, ignoring the noise of the television.

"What about your qualifications, Dr. Bennett, for this position?" a woman asked.

Bennett looked somewhat pained, then bored. The governor folded his arms with a complacent smile, his eyes half closed, while Bennett performed. "Well, as many of you know, I've headed the governor's commission on child abuse for the past year. In addition, my work in social psychology and child psychology here at the university speaks for itself." He went on to list degrees and honors, then nodded toward the back of the room for the next question.

A thick voice scratched, echoing, across the room. "What is the status of the investigation into the death of your sister, Elizabeth Bennett?"

For a moment or two there was shocked silence. Suddenly Helen's television set emitted a volley of sound — cameras whirring and photographs being snapped, microphones swerving to one corner of the room. Helen sat down cross-legged on the floor near

26

the set and strained to hear. For a few seconds the screen blurred as the camera was adjusted. Then the figure appeared clearly. He was tall, thick-set, with dark hair cut unevenly, as if he'd taken up the shears himself — with questionable results. A dark leather jacket covered his bulky frame, its rich surface giving off a buttery sheen as he stood up.

"Malone, *Contra Costa Ledger*. I asked, sir, if there has been any progress made in the investigation of the death of your sister, Elizabeth Bennett." The reporter sat down again, nonchalant, apparently oblivious of the commotion he had just caused. Cameras and microphones lurched back to the dais where Bennett, now joined by the governor, stood in confusion.

Aware that he was being scrutinized, Bennett cleared his throat. Helen admired his slick recovery. No more than a split second slid by before Bennett was back on track. "I have every confidence that Berkeley's finest will resolve this tragedy quickly." In a public show of grief the governor's right-hand man glanced down, then lifted his eyes to stare balefully at the reporter who had dared to ask him such a question. "The subject of this press conference is not my family's sorrow but Project Nightlight. I'd be happy to answer any questions you may have on that subject."

Malone persisted. "Do you have any other information on the murder you can give us at this time?"

The patience on Bennett's face gave way to a hard veneer, although his voice remained calm and steady. He glanced behind him and the governor quickly stepped in with thanks to the press as he ushered Bennett away from the threat of microphones and television cameras. Then the voice of the announcer closed the piece with a mention of a Project Nightlight exhibit on view at the Clarion Hotel, and a fundraising benefit to be held the next evening.

During the commercial, Helen sat transfixed, staring at an image of shiny new cars racing across impossibly hilly roads in the rain. The man was familiar. She was positive she'd seen him somewhere before, and recently. The fact that he worked for the *Contra Costa Ledger* meant nothing to her — she didn't take the paper, which covered news in the bedroom towns east of Oakland. The reporter's appearance, a strange combination of outdated style and lazy carelessness, had nothing to recommend it, either. So why was she so sure she knew that face? She sat through the rest of the newscast, trying to fix Malone's features in her memory.

The buzz of the doorbell jerked her out of the trance. She stumbled her way into the tiny foyer, switching on lights and bumping into walls. Seeing Frieda through the peephole, she took a deep breath before opening the door.

"I knocked and rang and knocked!" Frieda complained. "Are you all right?"

"Yes, yes, fine." Helen followed her into the living room and quickly switched off the television. As the screen faded into black, she got a brief look at herself on its dark surface. Hair sticking every which way, rumpled clothes covering a body that was getting far too thin, dark circles lining the eyes. Hell, she looked as bad as her office did.

Frieda's gaze roaming over the room confirmed

that the house wasn't looking so hot, either. "It's been quite a while since I've been here," she said with a lame laugh, reaching down to pick up Boobella.

Helen refrained from responding with an exact count of months, weeks and days since her last visit. "I know," she finally said as she watched Boobella purr with pleased recognition of her old friend. "Here, let me make some room for you." Helen swept up the newspapers and set them down on the coffee table.

"No, no, it's okay. I can't stay long. Cecily is waiting for me."

At first Helen felt familiar rage and jealousy at the words, until memory flooded in. She suddenly knew where she'd seen Malone. Frieda was still talking as Helen thought. "I'm sorry, what did you say?"

"I was just wondering if I did the right thing by bringing Cecily to see you. Helen, are you sure you're okay?"

Helen began to laugh. "Yes, yes, I'm fine. Sorry, I've just realized something. Look, tell Cecily I'll do what I can. No promises — but I'll try."

Chapter Five

"That's all she said?" Cecily asked. "After the way she acted this afternoon?"

Frieda shrugged and slipped off her shirt. Her dark skin took on a sheen in the dim light of the hanging lamp as she walked through the cavernous studio, away from the bed where Cecily lay, to take another look at the painting in the corner. "Hey, I'm just the messenger," she said over her shoulder. "Helen said she'd take the case. She wants you to call her tomorrow to talk some more, sign a contract, stuff like that." Her voice trailed off as she bent over the canvas, inspecting it closely.

Cecily rose up on one elbow. "You two still have a special relationship, don't you?"

Frieda pivoted sharply. "Why do you ask?"

"It's okay," Cecily said, smiling. "I'm in love with you myself. If anyone can understand, I can."

Frieda turned back to the painting. "I don't think it's relevant."

Cecily stretched under the sheets, feeling their texture against her bare skin. "Actually, she's kind of cute, in a strong, silent way."

Cecily jumped up and strode to where Frieda crouched before her painting. "Was she good in bed?"

Frieda knocked Cecily's hand away from her breast, where it had begun to tease the nipple. "Cut it out. I'm trying to do something here."

"So am I."

"Come on, Cecily. I want to get this finished."

"At midnight?" Cecily sighed, turned away. She smiled and began to hum tunelessly to herself. The idea she'd had earlier flowered and spread in her mind as she watched the stiff, angry back of her lover. She could hardly wait for morning.

Lydia Bennett stared, unseeing, at the late-night talk show host as he pranced across a soundstage in a frenzy of unbelievable enthusiasm. Lydia twisted her robe more closely around her shivering limbs and instantly felt the familiar bite of pain in her shoulder. With a muttered curse she groped for the remote control, and the room was swiftly plunged into blackness.

Her thoughts were filled with images of her son's debacle at the press conference, replayed on the late news. For this edition, however, the station had spiced up the affair with a few moments of back story on the discovery of her daughter's body last week. Stock footage of People's Park, then a quick switch to the remnants of the Darcy Building, and late-night viewers would now have Robert Bennett forever associated with murder and with the homeless.

"Wonderful," Lydia spat into the empty room. "After all the work I've put into this." She saw the episode as no less than an attempt to destroy her son's credibility and ruin his chances for running for governor next year. A momentary vision of Liz threatened to swim up into her consciousness, but Lydia firmly pushed it back, deep behind her rage. Anger was the only thing that would help now — the only way to persevere. The thought coursed through her, a tangible, physical thing, keeping her rigid in her bed. The lack of sleep no longer bothered her, now. Grim and stiff, she waited for morning.

In another corner of the house, just as Lydia turned off her television set, a lamp flicked on, shining a bright white circle on the glossy surface of an oak desk. A pair of hands rifled through the papers piled on the desk, then shakily tried the drawers. They were stopped by a faint scratching noise that came from the French doors at the opposite end of the room.

A whisper followed the scratching. "Jane! Come on, Jane, let me in!"

"Shit!" Jane Bennett left the desk and hurried across the room. After tussling with the door, a slight figure entered and followed her back to the desk. He was thin to the point of emaciation, huddled in his jeans and T-shirt. A slight odor of stale sweat preceded him, as if he hadn't bathed for a day or two. "I've been waiting forever," he whined, wiping his red-rimmed eyes with a grimy hand. "Did you find the money?"

"Goddammit, John, I told you to wait! You'll have the whole house here in a minute. And no, I didn't find the money!" Jane began to arrange the papers back into a neat pile. "Did you really think Daddy would have it sitting here in an envelope or something? Shit, your brains really have fried."

"But, Jane —" The hand clutched at her arm and ended up with a fistful of sleeve. There were tears in his voice. "I'm feeling really bad. My old man won't give me any more money." He dropped her sleeve and ran both hands through his greasy hair, his eyes wide and wild. "What can I do, Janey? What can I do?"

Jane realized she had to get him out of there before he started making real noise. "The money must be at headquarters somewhere," she said, more to herself than to him. "Come on, let's go. After that press conference tonight, all we need is for Daddy to find us here." She took a quick look around the room, then, satisfied, steered John outside into the cold night air.

* * * * *

The Pfister household was still full of commotion at this late hour. Martin's mother was on the phone with one of her girlfriends, bemoaning her life. Martin could hear her drone on about her husband, his father. "And the underwear! It just pops out at me from all over the place." Although Martin was safe in his bedroom, he could imagine the gestures that would accompany the complaint — the weary closing of the eyes, one hand rubbing her forehead, the pained expression. In another part of the house, his father was still holding a half-empty beer can and belching his way through the late movie.

Martin had been a prisoner here ever since the police had questioned him. At first, all the attention was exciting. Now he could see that it was all a trap, like all the things adults had ever done to him. He muttered a litany of curses on Jeremy, Hallie, and that damned old building.

Unable to contain himself any longer, Martin nimbly leaped out of bed and soundlessly made his way to the closet. He adjusted the closet door so that the light he switched on wouldn't show out in the hallway outside. His parents always left him alone at night, but you never knew for sure. Cautiously, he pulled out his treasure.

The knapsack scraped across the floor. Sitting cross-legged in the light from the closet, Martin methodically disemboweled the canvas bag. No one, not Jeremy, not Hallie, not his parents — and certainly not the police — knew anything about the souvenir he'd lifted from the Darcy Building that day. The police had assumed it was his own. It

34

certainly looked like any ordinary bookbag a student would carry around.

Every night Martin went through this ritual, silently enumerating his stolen secrets. He was convinced that this knapsack had belonged to the woman he'd found there. Now, after watching the news tonight, he was dead certain. But what should he do with this find? As he turned the items from the bag slowly in his hands, an idea was born. He had to think about it really hard, though. Staring at each item, his mother's whine and his father's coughing faded and Martin gave in to a heady sense of power. He'd show them all, soon enough.

"I'm sorry, darling," Bob Bennett mumbled. "I just can't do it right now." He rolled away from Alice and sighed as he settled on his back in the huge bed.

Alice closed her eyes and gritted her teeth to contain the sigh of disappointment. "It's all right, Bob, really it is," she said softly, patting his hand. Dismayed, she felt his start at her touch, his reflexive attempt to pull away that was quelled instantly. "I know you're upset," she went on, ignoring the voice in her head that reminded her of the months that had gone by since he'd touched her.

"You're so wonderful, Alice. I don't deserve you."

The words were perfunctory — an old habit that refused to die. Their blank gentleness washed over her, tepid and flat. "Is it — is it Liz, sweetheart?"

"What do you mean?" The gentle voice hardened, and Alice felt him staring at her. "Is what Liz?"

"The reason you're so upset tonight, honey." She moved closer to him and tried to snuggle against his body. "What that man said at the press conference — raking it all up." She sighed deeply and edged even closer. "As if you had something to do with her death." The violence of his movement as he sprang from the bed startled her into crying out. She could make out his shape looming up in the darkness, towering over her.

"What the hell do you think you're talking about, Alice?" he hissed. "Who says I had anything to do with Liz? Hell, I hadn't even seen her in years. No one has." He sat down again on the bed, his back to her. "Jesus Christ, woman."

Alice managed to speak. "Bob, darling, please! I was just wondering what made that man say what he did today, that's all."

But Bob was talking aloud to himself, ignoring her. "Someone's head is going to roll at the police commissioner's office as soon as I find out who leaked this story to the press."

"Is that what you think happened?" Alice asked.

"What the hell do you think it was? It wasn't you, was it?" he asked, his words sneering and cold.

"Of course not." She reached out to stroke him, to soothe his fears, but he shook her off. The old familiar routine of hurt and rejection settled into place for another night. Alice turned away so he wouldn't hear her stifled sobs or feel her body shake with the effort to keep silent.

* * * * *

The Bennett house lay in a quiet cul-de-sac in the high-priced region of Berkeley behind the Clarion Hotel. A huge old oak conveniently hid Malone's beat-up Vega from prying eyes. Any drivers passing by would write it off as a student's car, parked here harmlessly while the youngster visited Mom and Dad and enjoyed all the comforts of home. It was a long night, especially in the cold and gloom of early spring, but the reporter was content. Every so often he pulled a bottle of Jack Daniel's out from under his seat and laced up his coffee thermos.

He'd had only a couple of swigs when Jane Bennett took off with her junkie boyfriend. After that, the house remained quiet. Still, he was pretty sure he'd caused quite a bit of excitement this afternoon. He chuckled again when he remembered the look on Bennett's face after he'd popped the fatal question. The bastard certainly hadn't expected that.

With a sigh Malone stashed the bottle and started up the car, giving it a minute or two to warm up. Nothing else would happen tonight. He turned the car around and headed for the Caldecott Tunnel and home.

Chapter Six

There was already a good crowd gathering at the Clarion Hotel, Project Nightlight's temporary headquarters, when Helen arrived there early the next morning. Some were members of the press, looking around with an eager, hungry air. Some were merely curious, wondering what all the fuss was about. A handful with serious expressions were studying informational leaflets and brochures.

Helen smiled to herself as she entered the Clarion's portals. The inn resembled a wedding cake, with its ersatz Swiss chalet turrets and brilliant white paint. She had always wondered what the interior of this place was like but had been certain she'd never be able to afford the rates.

Unfortunately there was such a crush of people that she got only a vague impression of the inn's overstated grandeur from its lofty ceilings and immense corridors. Placards on easels advertised the benefit to be held that evening. Weaving her way through the crowd she noted the wide variety of people the project had attracted. A wizened older woman with papery, pale skin was in animated conversation with a young black man in a navy suit and red tie. Helen noticed a sign next to the bank of elevators announcing that the office was on the second floor. Not wanting to intrude on Bob Bennett's territory just yet, she contented herself with watching the crowd and leafing through the brochures she'd picked up.

One explained how the project originated. It was largely the work of one man, Bob Bennett, with the assistance of his daughter, Jane. The back of the leaflet showed a photograph of the two. Dad stood in quiet confidence, facing the camera squarely. One well-shaped hand rested lightly on Jane's shoulder. The young woman was tense, her lack of ease caught in the cruel black-and-white of the camera's honesty. The pinched nose and unhappy lines around her eyes were beyond the reach of any touching up. There was only a dim echo of the serenity and self-satisfaction on her father's face.

"Can we help you?" Without realizing it Helen had strayed from the elevators and wandered in the direction of a long row of tables staffed by beaming, wholesome young women. Helen was momentarily struck by the uniform good looks and perfect smiles of the girls who handed out information and signed up subscribers.

"Just looking around," Helen responded. "I saw the press conference on the news last night. Sounds like your boss is in for a little trouble."

The young woman's pretty features clouded over but she managed to keep smiling. "Well, I don't think that it — I mean, that the — unfortunate accident — will stop anything on the project. And Mr. Bennett is just wonderful, the way he's able to keep on going through all this," she finished in a final gush of praise. One small hand reached for a long sheet as she spoke. "Would you be interested in subscribing to Project Nightlight? For a small donation you could become a lifetime member —"

Helen cut her off with a grin. "Not just yet, thanks. I just wanted to pick up some information."

Disappointed, the girl looked beyond her and immediately her face froze. Helen heard heavy steps behind her and turned around to be confronted by Jane Bennett. If anything, she looked harsher and more miserable than the photograph on the pamphlet.

"Excuse me," she said to Helen, leaning over the table to confer with the young assistant over some technical matter. Helen drifted off, tucking the papers she'd acquired into her shoulder bag, and went out the doors into the mid-morning sunlight. She checked her watch — it was just ten o'clock. Time for one more trip before she met with Cecily at the Darcy Building.

It took only moments to reach her destination. The Sherman Hotel was approximately one mile from the Clarion, yet they might have been on different planets. A few yards from the oak double-doors, street people lounged, turning their faces to the sun, then to her, hoping for some spare change. She skirted the huddle of the homeless and stepped inside.

The hotel's interior was murky. Helen breathed in the mingled fragrances of antiseptic and mildew as she approached the front desk. A dark-skinned young man, possibly from India or Pakistan, looked up with an anxious smile. Helen took a deep breath.

"I'm looking for a friend of mine. She's supposed to be staying in this place," she started in a belligerent tone.

"What is her name, please?" he said, the smile faltering a bit at her forceful manner.

"Liz Bennett. Come on, I don't have all day," Helen snapped.

Flustered, the clerk flipped through the file box where registration slips were kept. "I'm sorry, I don't see her name. Are you certain you have the right hotel, miss?"

Helen sighed and rolled her eyes. "Yes, I'm certain! What is wrong with you people? Dammit, no one speaks English anymore, nothing gets done right!"

"But her name is not here. She has not checked in —"

Helen made a show of gritting her teeth and restraining her anger. "Look, pal, she was supposed to be here Tuesday night. That's right, last Tuesday. I don't suppose you could find yourself capable of looking back a week ago?"

The thin fingers fluttered through the slips again,

and he smiled and stammered. "I'm so very sorry, miss, but as you see I cannot find it."

"I've had enough of this crap from foreigners. When the hell did you get off the boat? I want to talk to the manager!"

He darted away, leaving the box out on the counter. With a sigh of relief Helen turned the box around and quickly looked through the records of the previous week. Not a trace of Liz Bennett. She didn't think the woman would have registered under an assumed name, or there would have been an indication of it in her letter to Cecily. Helen tried to imagine why Cecily would have refused to meet with her aunt. The kid's behavior was very confusing. Did she love her aunt? Hate her? Why bother to engage a private detective if she hated the woman? And why had Liz never checked into the hotel?

Lost in these thoughts, Helen looked up to see a heavy-set man with enormous bags under his eyes staring at her wearily. She noted his protective hand on his clerk's shoulder, the tired resignation in his voice. "I understand there's some confusion here," he started. "Mukesh says you were looking —"

Helen smiled, and the clerk and his boss both stared at the transformation from furious bitch to apologetic stranger. "I'm sorry. It's all my mistake. Please forgive my outburst," she tossed over her shoulder as she walked out.

"Thank God that's over," she muttered, opening her car door. "I hate being the heavy all the time." She pointed the car toward the Darcy Building and her appointment with Cecily.

Chapter Seven

Cecily was waiting at the Darcy Building when Helen arrived. The young woman was clearly nervous. Feet tapping impatiently, arms tight across her chest, she kept glancing around her. As Helen walked closer, she could see that the strongest emotion expressed on those pale features was anger.

"Sorry I'm late," Helen said as she stepped off the crumbling sidewalk and up to the building. "Traffic was really bad this morning."

"Why the hell you wanted to drag me here, I

don't know," Cecily snapped. "Couldn't we have done this in your office?"

Helen shrugged, interested to see that she'd gotten some kind of response from her. She was actually enjoying Cecily's discomfort. "Thought it might help for both of us to see the scene of the crime."

"Well, I think it sucks." Helen followed Cecily as she made awkward progress across the stubbly landscape of what had once been a manicured lawn. They paused at the entrance. "The place will probably fall down around our heads, you know."

"I think it will stand long enough for us to take a look." Helen switched on her flashlight as she ducked through the doorway, feeling ashamed. So what if the girl was sleeping with Frieda? Bringing her here was stupid and vindictive. Helen was better than that — she hoped.

"I'm not even sure where they found her. The police never took us here." Cecily spoke in a whisper, as if intimidated by the dark, dank interior of the building.

Helen swung the beam of her flashlight around what had once been the foyer. The light shone briefly on a small shiny object. It took only a moment for Helen to recognize it. "It must have been over here." She led the way to the corner, walking cautiously. Cecily crouched close behind her as Helen fingered the tattered remnant of bright yellow tape that indicated the recent presence of the police. She let it fall, fluttering, against the doorjamb.

Cecily backed away. "You go ahead," she said,

44

shaking her head. "I'll be right here." Chagrined, Helen nodded and stepped into the tiny room.

She saw that it was no bigger than a large closet. A sweep of the flashlight revealed that that was in fact its function. Impossible to tell how much the mess that confronted her had been created by the police and how much had been there before the discovery of the body. Anything bearing bloodstains or fingerprint evidence, anything that might have been used as a weapon, would, of course, have been long since removed.

Helen backed out of the closet and said, "I can't figure out what she would have been doing in this place." Cecily, obviously relieved at her emergence from the closet, waited quietly. "The letter said she'd be staying at the Sherman Hotel, right?"

"That's right."

"She never got there. To the Sherman Hotel, I mean." Her eyes accustomed to the gloom, Helen studied Cecily's face. "Why didn't you go there to meet her? She'd come a long way to talk to you. Didn't you want to see her? It had been year —"

"I couldn't have cared less! She ran off and left me and never came back! Served her right to be stood up, just like she did to me!" Cecily wiped a hand across her cheek and turned away, leaning against a wall. "I think I must have hated her, after all."

Helen moved closer. "Talk to me about her. I have to know."

Cecily sighed. "You know, I'm supposed to look like her."

"Really?"

Cecily nodded, looked down at her shoes. Her arm brushed against Helen's as she settled more comfortably against the gritty stone. "We don't have any pictures of her, even. It's as if she died before she died, somehow."

"What about the rest of your family? How have they reacted to all this?"

Cecily laughed, a sharp, bitter sound. "Reacted? Well, I'd hardly call it reacting. Granny and Dad are too caught up with the project and the governor. Mother and Jane are too caught up with Daddy." Her voice changed into a tremulous thread. "I guess I was the only one left."

"And what made you different from the others?"

"You don't like me very much, do you? Is it because of Frieda? I already know you were lovers."

Helen felt her face burning. She waited before answering, to keep her voice from revealing her feelings. When she spoke, her words cut through the dark like sharp-edged ice. "So far, Ms. Bennett, you haven't given me one good reason why you're so concerned. By your own admission, you never really knew your aunt. Your family had, for some reason, practically thrown her into exile. Why all the sudden interest, after all these years?"

Even though Helen was unconsciously trying to back away, Cecily moved even closer. Helen could feel the heat of the younger woman's body near her own. "If I told you, you'd just laugh at me. You'd think, poor little rich girl, feeling sorry for herself, spoiled brat."

Helen snorted. "What I think doesn't matter. Anything would be better than what you've been telling me — or rather, not telling me — up to now."

"Fine." Cecily moved away abruptly, causing a few drifts of dust to separate from the wall and sift over Helen's shoulders. "I don't know if you could understand what it's like to be, shall we say, different, in a family like mine. Pillar of the community, example of the perfect nuclear family, all that shit. Then along comes a freak like me."

Helen felt a sudden deep pain, remembering what it was like growing up in a small town in Mississippi. How she had fought against having to wear frilly dresses and attend local dances. How her own father threw her out right after high school. She was grateful for the darkness as she answered, "I get the picture."

"Well, all I remember is how Aunt Liz used to take my side whenever she was around. When I was little, that is. Later, once I understood what was different — how I'd always been attracted to women — she used to write and tell me not to worry, not to let the family get me down. She kept telling me she'd visit soon, but she never did." Cecily laughed. "She used to take me out for ice cream when I was little. I always had strawberry." The cool reserve came back into her voice as she added, "Sounds infantile, huh?"

Helen cleared her throat. "No, it doesn't. She gave you love and affection. Seems to me like you didn't get much of that growing up."

Cecily took another step away from Helen. "There — enough sob story for one morning. You asked for it."

Helen's response was cut short by a loud crash from just outside the building. Without thinking Helen grabbed Cecily by the arms and moved protectively in front of her. One hand groped to her side in search of a gun that wasn't there — a hangover from her old days as a cop. With a muttered curse, Helen forced herself to stay still as she listened intently. The room darkened as a cloud passed over the sun, filtering out what light had reached into the room.

Footsteps crunched on broken glass and rock outside. "What the hell is going on? You're hurting my arm," Cecily gasped into Helen's ear.

Helen felt her skin tingle as Cecily's warm breath moved over her neck. She was sharply aware of the girl's slender softness as she yielded to Helen's firm grasp. "Sorry," Helen mumbled, loosening her fingers. Cecily moved closer. Her chest rose and fell perceptibly, brushing Helen's back. "Someone is moving around out there. Probably just one of the transients from the park." The footsteps faded. Still holding Cecily, Helen pulled both of them out of the Darcy Building back into welcome light and air. No one was lurking near the entrance. In the distance a group of four men squatted on the ground around a pile of clothing, sorting out suitable garments.

"Jesus H. Christ! What the hell kind of shit is this, anyway?" Cecily's words were harsh, but they were shouted in fear. She tore away from Helen's hand with an extra obscenity thrown in for good measure.

Helen started to speak, then peripherally caught the movement of a car. The green soiled Vega raced down Dwight toward Telegraph, leaving behind the acrid stench of burning rubber. Malone, Helen thought, remembering the reporter from the press conference. He hadn't gone more than a block before Helen heard his brakes screeching. She and Cecily raced across the dirt-strewn lawn of the Darcy Building. Helen's heart pounded. She wasn't at all sure what she would see.

Fortunately, no macabre scene awaited them. A circle of men and women in bedraggled attire chanted and carried signs with slogans, all referring to People's Park. Helen saw one rotund man, wearing dirty jeans held up by a rope, attempt to hand Malone a sheet of paper — perhaps a petition, or some sort of flyer — through the open window of his car. The man snatched his hand away as the window rolled up, threatening to take off a few fingers with it.

Helen saw but didn't hear the shouted exclamation at this sign of hostility. While she watched, she was hurrying to her own car. Cecily trotted close behind.

"What now?" Cecily wailed, her slight form barely keeping up with Helen. "Listen, if it's all the same to you, I'd rather —"

"Shut up and get in the car," Helen ordered. To her surprise, Cecily meekly did so. Helen revved the engine, coaxing the aging vehicle to life. "We just might have a chance to follow this guy and see what he's up to."

Cecily braced herself against the passenger seat and stared ahead of in amazement. "The guy in that green bomb? But who is he?"

Helen ignored her as she pulled the car away from the curb, eliciting a cacophony of horns and offended shouts from drivers and pedestrians. By the time she reached the corner where Malone had been delayed, the motley group of protesters had just broken rank, allowing him to pass through and head toward the downtown area.

Helen glanced at her stunned passenger. "Put on your seatbelt. We're going for a ride."

Chapter Eight

Telegraph Avenue, at the best of times, was not the easiest street in Berkeley to traverse. Now, in the middle of a spring morning, crowded with cars and cyclists and various people on foot, it was a maze of extraordinary complexity. To make matters worse, a confusing pattern of one-way streets could induce rage in the most placid motorist. Helen grimly realized that Malone knew these streets as well as she did. With the ease of long habit he wove about the two narrow lanes that led farther and farther away from the center of the city. Helen was certain he'd picked up her car in his rear-view mirror, but there was nothing she could do about that.

Cecily's hands were clenched white as she gripped her seatbelt, her gaze fixed straight ahead in a caricature of anger and fear, as if she didn't know whether to rant or cry. "Do you mind," she said through gritted teeth, "telling me what the fuck is going on? Or are you hoping to get voted lunatic of the month?"

Helen neatly avoided running into a delivery van and changed lanes, keeping Malone's dusty car in view in the block ahead. "You don't recognize the guy in the car?" she asked calmly.

"Afraid not," Cecily responded.

"He certainly knows who you are, though. All the Bennetts, I expect."

"Look, I've had about enough —"

"The reporter at the press conference who asked about your aunt." Helen turned at Cecily's silence and saw the slow dawn of recognition replace the mask of fright. "He followed you up to my office yesterday afternoon. I saw him drive away when you and Frieda left. Then there he was on the television screen last night."

"My God. You're right. I didn't realize —" Cecily broke off and stared out the windshield. "How long has he been following me around?"

"No idea. You're sure you can't remember seeing him anywhere else?"

"No, never."

By now they were gaining on the Vega. Malone sped up, dodging cars that clogged Telegraph's wider lanes into Oakland. Then the inevitable happened —

a huge snarl met them at Ashby Avenue, the main artery from Contra Costa County into Berkeley. The usual tangle of cars was accompanied by honking horns and gesticulating drivers.

Helen managed to position her car in the far right lane while Malone was stuck in the left lane, pinned in on both sides by through traffic and by cars bound for the left-turn area. From what Helen could see, Malone was craning his neck, searching for a way to get around the knot of cars and escape the intersection, in order to continue on down Telegraph into downtown Oakland. Once there, Helen knew, it would be much easier for him to disappear than here in the web of Berkeley. He'd also have a better chance of hopping onto a freeway.

"Maybe we can go around on one of these side streets?" Cecily ventured timidly.

"And do what?" Helen snapped, frustrated. "We have to keep him in sight. I don't know which way he's going to turn next."

Cecily, as if regretting her attempt at conversation, cowered in her seat, her eyes wide with anxiety. Helen promised herself that she'd apologize later. She looked up just as the light changed. A horn blaring behind her nudged her forward through the intersection.

The crash came just as Helen made it to the opposite side. Behind her, metal sheared on metal and rang through the air with a sickening shriek that covered Cecily's high-pitched scream. Helen steered her car into the vacant lot that edged Ashby just past Telegraph. "Stay here," she commanded Cecily — a needless admonition. The girl showed no inclination to move from her seat.

The sight that met Helen was a repeat of so many scenes from her past, both in uniform and in plainclothes. The odd smell of scraped metal and fumes that was somehow hot, confusing to the senses, brought back grisly memories. The crowd shoved aside as Helen, under the powerful influence of adrenaline, pushed her way through. She got a peripheral impression of a man running up to a phone booth at a nearby gas station. After a quick scan of the scene for injuries, Helen was amazed and relieved to see that everyone was walking and apparently quite sound — no blood in sight.

Still in cop mode, she approached Malone's crumpled Vega. Miraculously, the only other car damaged appeared to be a silver Cadillac of ancient make. With dread spreading up from the pit of her stomach, Helen watched two men slowly pull Malone out of what remained of his car.

"What the hell happened here?" A woman standing next to Helen asked the question aimlessly, looking around her in a daze.

"That guy right there —" A man a few feet away pointed out Malone, who was now sitting on the ground and shaking his head — "he pulled right out from the turn lane and tried to get through the intersection in front of everyone else."

"Idiot." "Asshole." "Where do these fools learn to drive?" "He isn't bleeding, is he?" "I think he's okay. Just shook up." "Hell, I thought he was dead." The voices surged around Helen. All eyes were fixed on Malone, who was now trying to stand up.

"Dammit, take your paws offa me!" Malone pushed away a helping hand and lumbered awkwardly to his feet. "Shit, leave me the fuck alone." The crowd watched as he stood, weaving and holding one hand to his head. In the distance, sirens wailed, drew near.

Helen suddenly realized how close they were all standing to the wreckage. "Come on, we should get away from this thing," she called out. "It could blow anytime." Now that they saw there was no corpse to gawk at, people nodded in agreement and started to shuffle away. Helen steered those she could manage, her arms stretched out protectively. Slowly, she was clearing the area.

Malone was leaning heavily on the man who'd spoken to Helen earlier. Together they limped toward the ambulance that had just made its appearance. To the general enjoyment of all, a fire truck added its bright color and flashing lights. Somehow the driver of the truck backed the huge vehicle onto the edge of the vacant lot where Helen had hurriedly parked her own car. She glanced back and saw Cecily standing in an air of uncertainty next to the car. She waved at Helen, her face scared. She started across the street, but Helen waved her back with an angry gesture.

"Not right now, idiot," Helen muttered under her breath. She took one last look at Malone, who was disappearing inside the ambulance.

"Hey!" One of the firemen hopped off the back of the truck, his black coat flapping against his boots. "Get away from that car!"

"Right," Helen called back. She was turning away reluctantly when she stumbled over the notebook. On its cheap cardboard cover she saw the name

BENNETT stenciled with a thick-nubbed magic marker.

"Come on, lady, this is dangerous! Get out!" Two more firemen had joined the first. They tromped heavily over the asphalt toward the Vega.

"Okay, guys. Sorry." Helen trotted back to her own car, where Cecily, with shaking hands, beat a nervous pattern on the hood. "Let's go," Helen said. She slid into the driver's seat, started the engine, and tossed the notebook over her shoulder onto the back seat. Cecily's mouth fell open but she obeyed. "I'm taking you back to the Darcy so you can pick up your car."

"Is that all you have to say?"

Helen smiled. She was, for some reason, enjoying the shock on Cecily's face. "What do you want me to say?"

"I can't believe this. Are you pretending you're in a movie or something? Christ, a man practically gets killed in front of us, some weirdo is stalking me and my family, and you just drive around like you're going out for a six-pack or something! Jesus." She flopped against the seat for emphasis, closing her eyes.

"Not a six-pack."

"What?"

"It's more likely to be bourbon. Didn't Frieda tell you I prefer hard liquor?"

"It's none of your goddam business what she told me. Just keep driving, all right?"

Helen stopped the car at nearly the same location she'd used before in front of the ruined building. The same protesters were there, handing out the same flyers. "Do you want me to tear up the contract you signed yesterday?"

Cecily opened the door and put one foot out on the ground. After a moment's silence she said, "No, not yet, I guess."

Helen snorted. "That's hardly a glowing, enthusiastic response. You sure you want me on this case?"

"No more high-speed chases?"

Helen held up her hand. "Only when necessary. Scout's honor."

Cecily nodded. "Like I said — you'll do for now. Oh, I almost forgot." She dug something from her jacket pocket and tossed it onto Helen's lap. "A ticket for the benefit at the Clarion tonight. Try not to get killed before it starts."

"What should I wear?" Helen asked, slipping the envelope onto the dashboard.

A faint grin appeared on Cecily's face. "Well, it is supposed to be rather formal, but don't get dressed on my account." She backed away, hesitated, then said, "You know, Frieda never really talks a lot about you."

"Well, I don't know if that's good or bad."

"So I guess I have to figure you out all by myself." Then she was gone.

Helen waited until her car was out of sight before she reached behind her and groped for the notebook that had fallen out of Malone's Vega. She knew she should get back to the office with this, but the temptation was too great to resist just one quick look. The quick look stretched into several minutes of disturbing reading. Only the persistence of the

band of protesters, tapping on her window, forced
her to find her way back to Shattuck and the safety
of her office.

Chapter Nine

The benefit at the Clarion Hotel for Project Nightlight was in full swing when Helen arrived. She stood, waiting, at the edge of the crowd, near a huge faux marble pillar. Around her the mass of people surged and swarmed. It was a different set than the ones she'd seen here earlier. This morning's visitors to the Clarion had been a combination of the curious and the devoted. Tonight the unifying factor was money. The program ought to do well financially, Helen thought. Nearby was the sign indicating Bennett's temporary headquarters on the second floor. No one in the crowd seemed interested in it at the moment.

"Here you are." The familiar voice roused her from her thoughts. Cecily handed Helen a fresh drink. Helen swirled the bourbon around in the glass, then savored the sharp taste of liquor hitting the back of her throat. It melted like molten gold, and she immediately felt herself expand under its warmth. "Apparently," she said after her first swallow, "Malone has been keeping this file for several years."

"And the Bennett family is his main concern?"

"Yep." Helen finished the drink, decided she should wait a bit before searching out another. "Mostly your father, of course. A few things about the others. Lydia — your grandmother — shows up in society column stuff. Your mother does, too. And there've been a few things lately about Jane taking over the financial aspects of Project Nightlight." Helen fiddled with her glass and grinned at Cecily. "There's even an item about you."

"Me! I don't think I've ever been in the papers. Not once."

"Well, we're not talking mainstream here."

Cecily took a sip from her own drink and stared, puzzled, at Helen. "Then what, for Christ's sake?"

"What was your high school paper called?"

"You've got to be kidding."

"Nope. There you are, editor-in-chief of the *Claremont Gazette*. It even has a photograph." Helen looked down into her empty glass. "You haven't changed much."

"Well, it hasn't been all that long, you know."

The two women were silent, and Helen tried to take in the scene. It was not the sort of gathering to which she was accustomed. Project Nightlight attracted all kinds of people. University intellectuals, some of whom Helen knew by sight, chatted with the glitterati of high society. A few heavy-duty political types, obviously feeling out of place, wandered sheepishly among waiters bearing trays of hors d'oeuvres. Then there were the "suits" — vaguely official-looking business representatives, young and unmarred and fresh from corporate America. They seemed most at home in this oddly stilted environment.

Helen glanced down at her own blue suit, dug out from her hall closet and pressed in haste at the local cleaners. "I hope I look all right," she'd said to Cecily on arriving at the Clarion that evening. "This is not exactly everyday attire for me."

Cecily had ushered her past the muscular security guard who politely but thoroughly scrutinized her. "You look pretty good to me," Cecily said. "Blue is definitely your color."

"You should have seen me in uniform."

"I have." Cecily tossed a mischievous grin her way. "Don't look so shocked, Helen. Frieda has a couple of old photo albums in her studio. I found quite a few pictures of you this afternoon."

Helen stood near one of the buffet tables while Cecily sought out her first drink. She tried not to think about the odd feeling of pleasure she got from the mild flirtation Cecily offered. A few innocent words, a smile or two, and she was nervous. "Terrific," she breathed. Fortunately, the combination of Cecily, bourbon, and endless questions about Malone tided her over the first few minutes of conversation.

"I guess he's at home now?" Cecily was asking. "I mean, he didn't look all that damaged from the accident."

"Well, he's certainly going to wonder what happened to the notebook"

"You're sure it's all right?"

Helen had a moment's glimpse in her mind of the safe that rested beneath a group of dilapidated ferns in her living room. "I'm sure," she said.

"But why would he have that kind of information? Newspaper clippings, photographs, stuff about the project — what's he trying to do? It's so creepy." She shuddered as she finished her drink.

Helen looked at her, saw that she was disturbed, and decided not to tell her about everything else in the notebook. The pages full of venomous hate for Robert Bennett, the ugly drawings, the scribbled comments about perversity — all of that could wait for some other time. Instead, she said, "For some reason the man has an obsession with the Bennett family. Tomorrow I'll try to get in touch with him, snoop around the newspaper he works for, find out what I can."

Cecily groaned. "Uh-oh. Mother and Granny are headed this way." She looked at Helen, confused. "I'm not quite sure how I ought to introduce you."

"It can wait. I'll just wander around, get a look at things." Helen put on her best bland smile and turned to the tidbits arrayed on silver platters. Snowy white cloth draped the buffet tables. She'd munched her way through a few interesting concoctions when she saw another familiar face in the crowd.

He held a tall glass as he leaned against a wall near a set of double doors. The dark suit hid a taut, muscular body, and his handsome regular features turned many an eye, both male and female. Now and then he would smile at a passerby, but Helen saw that his eyes, deep-set and heavy-lidded, were actually in a continuous scan of the room. She edged her way slowly around the crowd and successfully avoided catching his notice until she stood next to him.

"Of all places to find Manny Dominguez, this is the last I would have figured," she said, standing at his side.

His mouth fell open in amazement, then widened in a grin. "Shit, Black, when did you join the ranks of high society?"

"I was about to ask you the same thing. The last time we worked together, they weren't paying cops enough to afford that suit. Unless, of course, you finally let your wife do the shopping."

"Are you jerking me around, Helen? I stole the suit. How the hell have you been anyway?"

"Getting along. You still in vice?"

"Back in homicide now. How's, uh, how's Frieda?" he asked, suddenly clumsy.

Helen shrugged. "Don't know. We're not seeing much of each other these days."

"Oh." Manny seemed confused, not certain how to respond to a situation that had always made him nervous when they were partners. "Too bad. I guess."

Helen helped him out. "Never mind about me. Is this visit official?"

He shook his head and rattled the ice in his glass. "Strictly off the record. Mike, one of the security guys, used to work for the department. I talked him into letting me in for a look around."

"What do you mean, off the record?"

He snorted. "The investigation into the death of one Liz Bennett is closed." He nodded at her amazement. "Yeah, I know. Bullshit." Manny lifted his glass and peered into it as if looking for an explanation in the ice cubes. "My guess is that Big Daddy Bennett said a few choice words to the governor and got the whole thing called off."

"So naturally they're sticking it to one of the transients from People's Park," Helen said. "Beautiful."

"What about you? Did you decide to get respectable? Come on, I showed you mine, now you have to show me yours."

"Please, not on an empty stomach. Not until you tell me what made you push your way in here."

Manny pursed his lips and kept staring into his glass. "Because the whole setup sucks, Helen. I beg for months to get out of vice, back into homicide, then I get the rug pulled out from under me by a bunch of fucking pencil-pushers. They're ready to write off Liz Bennett like so much garbage, after we busted our butts to identify her, to get some answers."

"Did you get any?" Helen asked.

"Not much. The M.E. places her death between seven and nine the night of Tuesday the fifteenth. Autopsy didn't reveal anything new. No drugs or alcohol."

Helen looked at the crowd of happy, healthy

well-off supporters of Bennett and the governor. "You're right, Manny," she finally said. "It sucks. Meanwhile, it's just one more reason to shove the homeless out of sight while palms get greased. You know they're going to turn this into a reason to push them farther and farther away."

Manny shot her a warning glance. "Look out. You're in a room full of politicians here. They might think you're giving a speech."

As if on cue, Bennett made his appearance amid spattered applause and half-hearted cheering. Helen recognized the governor just behind him, talking to a young woman in a too-short, ill-fitting gray suit. Helen recognized Jane Bennett, looking worse than she had this morning. An older version of Cecily, the few years that separated the sisters had taken a terrible toll on Jane, parching her pale skin and honing her features into sharpness. Helen remembered Malone's notes on the junkie boyfriend and felt a wave of pity for her.

While the group flocked around Bennett, a little girl in a painfully clean pink dress trotted up to him, followed by her mother, who wore a suit in the same bright shade of pink. Bennett, to the tune of clicking cameras, hoisted the girl into his arms and flashed a smiling face to the crowd. Applause broke out again. Manny groaned. "Oh God, she must be the only kid in the room. Who's he going to kiss next?"

Helen kept watching Bennett. He reached over the girl's head and gently twisted a strand of her shiny blond ponytail in a gesture that somehow combined authority and affection. A couple of microphones roved near him. "It's for kids like her

— like mine and yours — that Project Nightlight was started," he began in a loud clear voice. The rest of his words were cut off by the sound of gunfire.

Chapter Ten

It took several minutes for confusion to run its course and for the people in the assembly room to realize that the sound had come from outside the building. Manny and Helen, reacting instinctively, had already moved quickly in the direction of the shots. "Right out front," Manny muttered, one hand reaching inside his jacket for his revolver. Sirens and flashing lights were quick to greet the crowd that flowed through the doorway to the sidewalk.

Helen glanced over her shoulder and saw that a few security types had already surrounded Bennett.

A few yards behind Helen, Bennett had frozen, his hands clutching the little girl in his arms until her cries of pain apparently broke through his shock. Quickly — and none too gently — he dumped the child back in her mother's arms and reached out to the burliest of the bodyguards, who spoke into a walkie-talkie produced from under an oversized sports jacket. His eyes darted around the room as he whispered into it. Bennett bobbed fearfully behind him.

Helen grabbed Manny's arm. "Let's see if we can find out what's going on." Manny took a swift turn down a short corridor, then another turn, then led her into an alley behind the hotel. At the head of a dark, narrow passage stood a uniformed police officer. Manny called out a greeting. "Hey, Brad!"

"Lieutenant Dominguez? I didn't know you were here tonight." The young officer, so fresh from the academy that he squeaked and shone, looked doubtfully at Helen.

"Me neither, but life's full of surprises." Helen thought his profile handsome as he looked toward the street. "Looks like you guys got it under control. What the hell happened out here, anyway?"

"Some punk on PCP, I think. Bob McKenzie and Jim Drake are on top of it now. He's not such a big guy. They got him down pretty fast." Brad was still keeping one eye on Helen as he spoke. "Hey, Lieutenant, I thought you guys were off this thing now. I mean, everyone is going around saying —"

"Yeah, that's what I thought, too. Catch you later." And Manny smoothly moved them out of the alley into the main street. The other uniformed officers nodded at his familiar face and let it pass. Helen tried to remain inconspicuous while observing as much as she could.

Brad's voice pierced through the noise. "Move along there! Let's keep this way clear!" Helen looked over her shoulder and saw the young policeman gesturing at a small thin figure that hovered at the other end of the alley. In the dim light she couldn't see much — just that it was male, young, and skinny. The boy, who couldn't have been much younger than Brad himself, backed under a streetlamp. The bright circle of light revealed a face pitted with acne. He stared at them from behind thick spectacles, which he kept pushing back up the bridge of his nose. Brad started toward him with a purposeful stride, and the boy broke into a run. Helen saw him get into a bright red sports car and drive off in a big hurry. Feeling Brad's curious gaze on her, she joined Manny again.

Most of the crowd hovered near the main entrance, shuddering with delicious anticipation of the imminent arrest of some poor son-of-bitch who most clearly didn't belong there. As Manny conferred with a couple of officers he knew, Helen kept her place at the edge of the activity.

No one noticed her. All eyes were fixed on the young man writhing on the ground beneath the sturdy arms of two policemen. Another officer was carefully placing a handgun in a plastic bag. From where Helen stood, the gun looked like the ever-popular Midnight Special. The man groaned and mouthed something unintelligible. A feeble attempt to break away from the iron grip of the law was met by a slight twist to his hand that caused him to yield and cry out.

Helen heard a sharp intake of breath beside her. Jane clutched a fist to her mouth as she watched the would-be criminal lifted up and dragged unwillingly to a black-and-white. Then Cecily was there, appearing out of nowhere.

"Jane? Are you okay?"

But Jane flung her sister off with disgust. "Get off me, you fucking bitch." Unaware of Helen's presence, Cecily stared after Jane as she shoved her way back into the building. Helen started after her, leaving Manny behind.

Once the doors closed behind her, the tumult outside faded to a dull murmur. Bennett himself had disappeared, and only a handful of his proteges remained huddled near the buffet tables, sipping drinks and nibbling like rabbits on whatever was available. The waiters had vanished. A few eyes followed Jane as she went into a waiting elevator, but the hangers-on turned to food, drink, and speculation as Helen passed by. She heard someone shout, "Hey, they're taking him away!" The few people standing around emptied the room, pushing through the doorway.

Helen used the fire stairs she'd spotted near the elevators to get to the second floor. Bennett's temporary headquarters were clearly marked — a gilt-edged frame held the plaque announcing the home of Project Nightlight. Jane had foolishly left the door ajar, clearly unaware that Helen was right behind her. She must have figured on privacy while her boyfriend was creating a diversion downstairs.

Helen stood in the hallway listening. Papers shuffled, drawers slammed, and Jane breathed heavily in ragged spurts. Finally Helen could stand it no longer. She pushed the door open.

Jane's face glowed a sickly yellow in the circle of light shed by a desk lamp. The room itself was thrown into a weird series of shadows silhouetting file cabinets and desks. Rage and fear emanated from her. "What the hell are you doing in here? Who are you?"

"His name is Jack, isn't it? What's he on? Must be some pretty heavy stuff." Helen softly closed the door. Her voice was low but it seemed to escalate Jane's fear. "They won't hurt him," she continued as she crossed the room. "But they're sure going to ask him a lot of questions."

"Get out of here." Jane's voice shook and her hands clutched spasmodically at the currency she'd raked up from the open drawer. "If you don't I'll —"

"You'll what? Call the cops?" Helen leaned on the desk with both hands, her face drawing closer to Jane's. "I think they'd be pretty interested in talking to you. How's he been getting money for his little habits? Maybe Project Nightlight has been subsidizing them."

Jane's hands loosened and crisp green bills fell to the desk. She slumped into a chair that squealed under the sudden impact of her weight. "Are you with the police?" she asked, listless, her voice flattened with exhaustion.

Helen stood up straight. Jane's face receded into the shadows. "I'm a friend of Cecily's. And no, I'm not a cop."

71

Jane sat up, suddenly alert. "My God," she breathed. "Cecily said she — you're a private investigator, aren't you?"

To Helen's surprise, Jane started to laugh hysterically. The laughter soon turned to gasping sobs. Helen spotted a water cooler in the corner and forced Jane to drink two cupfuls. "Sorry," Jane said, setting the paper cup down on the desk.

"No need to be sorry."

"No?" Jane smiled wryly and shook her head. "Jesus. What now? Are you going to turn me in or something? Tell Daddy what a bad girl I've been?"

Helen looked down at Jane — her haggard face, the tired green eyes, the tremors that flowed through her clumsy hands. "I'm not sure. That depends."

"On what?"

"On what you tell me about your Aunt Elizabeth."

"She's dead. There's nothing to tell." Jane was sullen, her voice a dull monotone.

"Fine. Let's talk to your father. Maybe he can tell me a few things about Liz, and I can tell him a few things about you." Helen strode to the door and held it open.

"No! Please — come back. What — what do you want to know?"

Relieved at this easy success, Helen stayed near the door. "You tell me. Why did she die?"

"I don't know, I don't know! All I know is she was talking to Dad a week ago, and then she was dead."

"A week ago, exactly? Last Tuesday?" The day

she'd asked Cecily to meet her, the same day she died.

Jane was babbling, close to falling apart. "I didn't know who it was — he meets with a lot of people — it was just this woman talking to my father in this office. Nobody seemed to know anything about her. Then later I realized it had to be Aunt Liz. It's not my fault — I hadn't seen her since I was a kid!" She stood up and came near Helen. "It's not my fault!"

Helen grabbed her by the shoulders to calm her down. "No one is saying it's your fault. Did you tell the police?"

Jane shrugged, shook her off. "I told them. I don't think they cared. What does it matter, anyway?"

Helen tried to think what this visit from Liz could mean. "What happened? Did they fight, or —"

"I tell you, I don't know! And I don't give a damn! The woman disappeared when I was a kid, and I never knew her." Jane went back to the desk, slammed the drawer shut, and slung a purse over her shoulder. "They talked, all right? And now if you'll excuse me I have to go."

"Going to try to buy Jack's way out of jail?"

With a look of contempt, Jane shoved by her. Helen absently turned off the lamp and went back into the hall only to find Frieda looking at her in surprise.

Chapter Eleven

It was nearly ten-thirty when Frieda turned her car into Helen's street. Helen resolutely looked out of the passenger window, glad that the darkness partially concealed her embarrassment. She hadn't noticed how low her tires were, and now she was afraid that Frieda would think she'd engineered the whole thing so that she could maneuver Frieda into her house. "I'm sorry about this," she said for the tenth time.

"Good grief, Helen. You don't have to keep apologizing about it. I wasn't going to leave you stranded there." Helen couldn't be sure, but Frieda actually sounded pleased. Was it altruism, or just the enjoyment of having the upper hand for once? "We can still be friends, you know."

The car stopped in Helen's driveway. "Thanks a million," Helen said. She hurriedly opened the door while the engine was still running. "I guess I'll get the car towed or something tomorrow."

"Hey, wait." Frieda opened her door and stepped out. "Can I come in for a second?"

Helen led the way up the walk, her nerves on edge. "Careful," she cautioned. "I forgot to turn on the porch light when I left tonight."

"Same old Helen," Frieda laughed. "You never could remember to do that." Helen fumbled at lights in the hallway while Boobella ecstatically greeted Frieda, their reunion loud and joyous. "You okay back there?" Frieda called.

"Uh, yeah, fine." Helen quickly folded the envelope she'd found on the floor where someone had slipped it under the front door. There was no time to look at this mysterious message now. It slid easily into her jacket pocket, its thin crackling tempting her. She strode into the living room, where Frieda, a very contented cat slung over her arm, stood waiting.

Helen switched on a lamp or two, not yet willing to look directly at Frieda. "Would you like a drink, or something? I think there's some whiskey in the kitchen." She busied herself with straightening pillows and rearranging newspapers while Frieda's gaze followed her around the room.

"I think I'll just use your bathroom," she finally said. Boobella, deposited unceremoniously on the floor, emitted a meek protest and stalked off into inner regions. Helen stood uncertainly in the middle of the room. She thought she knew Frieda well — she thought she recognized the extra warmth in her voice, the glow of her eyes. Surely she was mistaken this time. After all, Frieda couldn't possibly want her again, not when she had young, nubile Cecily Bennett waiting for her.

Noises coming from the direction of the bathroom goaded Helen into action. She took off her jacket and made for the bedroom. After making sure the envelope was still safely concealed, Helen hung up the jacket, shut the closet door, and turned around to find Frieda standing inches away. "What are you doing here?" Helen blurted.

Immediately she regretted the harsh tone her words had taken. Frieda backed away, arms folded. Her face froze. "Sorry. I just wondered where you went."

Helen then moved without thought, without conscious choice. "I'm sorry. That sounded rude." Her hand reached out to Frieda, but the other woman avoided Helen's touch.

"No, no, you're right. I don't have any right to be here. Not now."

Helen was moved by the bitterness in Frieda's voice. "That's not it at all, Frieda," she said gently. "Look, there's nothing I'd like better than to ask you to stay here with me for the night. But you have someone else waiting for you."

"Cecily?" Helen was taken aback by the sharp way Frieda said the name. "Let's just say that she and I have an understanding. We both do what we want with our lives. No commitments, no promises."

Frieda sat on the bed and ran her hands through

her hair. Helen watched as her arms lifted, revealing her thin torso against the dim light of the lamp.

Frieda said, "We're very open about it with each other."

"Unlike you and me," Helen said, smiling ruefully.

"Oh, come on! We were never 'married,' Helen." Frieda laughed, regaining some of her confidence.

"No?" Helen sat down gingerly on the bed, near but not too near. "It felt like a marriage to me, Frieda. And when you left it felt like we were being divorced." One hand smoothed the bedspread next to Frieda's leg. "You're not an easy woman to forget."

"Neither are you." Frieda leaned over to embrace Helen.

Starved by months and months of self-denial, Helen was overwhelmed and unable to resist. For a moment or two, she tried to persuade her body to turn away, to stop herself before it was too late. But it was just too much. Frieda's skin, her long thick hair trailing over Helen's arms, the scent of her neck, were impossible to refuse. She felt the slight pressure of Frieda's body, its bones so much smaller than her own.

"My God, I've missed you," Frieda whispered. "I used to dream about being with you like this again." She let the full weight of her body fall on Helen, her breasts moving against Helen's with only thin fabric between them. Slowly Frieda shifted so that the motion created a slow, teasing rhythm.

Helen moaned and pulled Frieda's head down close to her own, lacing her fingers into Frieda's hair. When their lips met Helen kissed her with a savagery she hadn't even known she'd kept hidden for all those months. Their tongues melted against each other, caressing and thrusting, and Helen felt Frieda tremble.

They managed to sit up and undress, looking shyly away from each other as if exposing themselves for the first time. Fingers fumbled at buttons, clothes were tossed into awkward heaps. Helen reached for the lamp as Frieda slipped beneath the sheets.

Helen laughed. "I feel really nervous. Like some idiotic blushing bride."

"You don't have to be afraid of me. We know each other pretty well," Frieda murmured as she nestled into Helen's side.

Helen turned to her warmth. Her mouth grazed Frieda's neck, her tongue stroking the small delicate ear. Frieda sighed as Helen's palm gently circled her breast and began a kneading motion, as if testing the weight and size of it. Against her legs Helen felt the heat flowing from between Frieda's thighs. Frieda stroked Helen's back until her hands progressed across Helen's belly and made their way to the thatch of dark curly hair that was now damp with arousal. Helen could not suppress a small cry of pleasure as Frieda slid her fingers deep inside, probing, urgent, demanding response.

Helen had never reached climax so quickly before. Moments after Frieda's hand touched her, Helen's body shook with orgasm, muscles fluttering.

When the spasms stopped, Helen moved so that her legs straddled Frieda's shoulders, her hands parted Frieda's legs, and her tongue reached into the bittersweet flesh hidden there. She felt Frieda's warm mouth, and she pushed her hips against the gentle pressure from Frieda's tongue, darting in and out. Slowly at first, their bodies moved together, twisting and arching as their need increased.

Frieda came first, crying out sharply in the way Helen remembered so well, taking her mouth away from Helen as she let her head fall back against the pillows. Helen tasted her climax, savoring it as Frieda moaned and her muscles relaxed. Then Frieda moved forward again, teasing and insistent. Helen shifted her hips lower and the sudden sensation of Frieda's tongue on the delicate skin brought her swiftly to release. She sank, tired but tremendously happy, against Frieda's legs. Neither one spoke or made a sound but continued to stroke and caress.

Sometime later, half asleep, Helen roused herself enough to move her weight off Frieda, sliding under the sheets and curling her body to match Frieda's form. Frieda murmured something, then sighed, slipped Helen's arm around her waist and relaxed her back into Helen's side. As they lay there, spent and motionless, Helen kept drifting close to sleep, then suddenly snapping to attention. It was useless, she realized, listening to Frieda's deep heavy breathing. She wouldn't be able to relax until she had a look at it.

Slowly, carefully, she eased her arm away from the woman sleeping beside her. Frieda made no sound as Helen lifted the sheets and slipped cautiously from the bed. The closet door groaned faintly as Helen opened it. She groped for her jacket and found it quickly. Still naked, Helen padded out of the bedroom and took the jacket into the bathroom.

The handwriting on the plain envelope, an

ordinary business size, was completely unknown to her. Her name was scrawled in block letters across its surface, and there was no return address in the upper corner. With a mixture of eagerness and trepidation, Helen lifted the flap and drew out a single sheet of paper. It had been ripped from a legal pad, its top edge serrated unevenly. She unfolded the sheet.

I know you have the notebook. Call me at the paper. Malone.

Chapter Twelve

He looked none the worse for wear when Helen
saw him the following morning. A deep graze over
one eye, a bruised cheek, and thick bandages
swathed around his left wrist — other than these
signs of recent catastrophe, Frank Malone appeared
to be the same unkempt middle-aged man he'd been
a couple of nights ago. Helen could tell with
accuracy what he'd eaten for breakfast by reading
the omens left on his tie and shirt-front.

A telephone receiver was wedged between ear
and shoulder as he watched her walk into the office

he shared with another reporter at the *Contra Costa Ledger.* Malone's voice grated and grumbled, but somehow it was warmer, more human, than what Helen had heard on television.

He studied her in silence, and Helen had a glimpse of his bloodshot eyes. "Later," he mumbled into the receiver. He hung up, never taking his eyes off her. "Christ, what the hell kind of hours you keep? I shoved that note under your door at ten and you were still out. Then you have the balls to call me up at six o'clock this morning." He shook his head and waved his unswathed hand in an absurd courtly gesture, toward a chair.

Helen sat down, her mind fleeting back for a moment to six o'clock — how she hadn't wanted to stick around and witness yet another grand exit from Frieda. Instead she'd called up the newspaper on the off chance that someone could get a message to Malone first thing. "I didn't think you'd be here so early," Helen said. "You probably ought to be resting, after what you've been through."

Malone let loose with an odd noise, something between a snort and a guffaw. "Shit, I do my best work at night. Or so my editor tells me, when he's not riding my ass about deadlines." He clasped his huge hands over his belly and leaned back in his swivel chair, forcing a groan from the casters that held his bulk. "So, what do I have to do to get my notes back?"

"All you have to do is talk to me, Malone. Answer a few questions."

"A few questions," he repeated. "I don't enjoy that very much. Goes against the grain."

Helen shrugged, got up and headed for the door.

"Then we're both wasting time." But Malone, surprisingly swift, heaved himself from the chair and stood in the entrance, one arm extended against the doorjamb.

"All right, all right. It can't be that bad, even from a private eye. Go on, sit down, we'll talk."

They returned to their seats, Malone first closing the door. Helen started talking before he got back to his desk.

"Why have you been following me around?"

He looked relieved, as though he'd been expecting something else. "I haven't. I've been following Cecily Bennett around."

"Why?"

"Probably for the same reason she hired you. I want to know what happened to Liz." His eyes dropped from her direct gaze and his thick fingers drummed against the desk. One hand reached up to tug at his greasy mustache. "I don't buy the official story any more than that kid does."

"Why not?" Helen asked, stiffening against the sympathy she was beginning to feel for him.

Malone's mouth twitched. When he answered, his voice was tender, all trace of whiskey-soaked bitterness gone. "Liz never got a fair shake in life. Not from her family, not from schools or work or —" He broke off, slammed a drawer shut. "Hell, I was just hoping I could do this one thing for her, find out what really happened."

"You loved her," Helen said softly.

But the moment of vulnerability vanished. "Any other questions? Or do I have to do something drastic to get my notes back?" he snapped.

"You haven't earned them yet. Look, I'm not

going to get anywhere on this case unless I know something about the victim. So far she's a complete mystery. Tell me about her."

"Then I get them back?"

"We'll see."

"Fuck, you must be related to the editor. Steel *cojones*." Malone sighed and positioned his chair so that his face was turned away. He spoke in such low tones that Helen strained to hear him. "I met Liz when we were both going to Cal. She was going to be a social worker. I was convinced I'd be the next Mencken. Jesus. Well, there we were, living together back in the summer of love. Hell, I didn't know anything about her family for months, not until big brother was in the papers about some new study on child abuse." He laughed bitterly at the memory. "I'll never forget it. She saw that article one morning and just went crazy. Flipped out, crying, hysterical — I'd never seen anything like it. It took me all day to persuade her to talk to me. Then all she would say was that that was her brother."

"She didn't tell you anything else? Why the article upset her so?"

"What did I just say? No, she wouldn't talk about it. Then she got really sick. I mean, *sick*. Throwing up. Christ, most kids get worked up over their family, but this was fucking nuts."

Helen waited, but Malone remained silent. "Then what?" she finally asked.

"Then she left." Malone moved slowly in the chair until he faced Helen again. "Up and left like a bat out of hell, about a month after the article. I came home one night and everything was gone. Just a check to help pay the rent for the next month." Even now his eyes shone with grief at the memory. "Look, I know I sound full of shit. That was years ago. And I've done my share of screwing around since then. But I've never met a woman like her. Who'd put up with me, tell me I was worth something, make me believe in myself. Ah, what the fuck. What the fuck."

"Did you ever hear from her again?"

He coughed a couple of times before answering in a low voice. "A couple of letters and postcards. She never gave me a way to get back in touch with her, though. I wasn't going to chase her down, or anything — I just wanted to see her again."

"Where were the letters from?"

He looked at her and sighed. "I think I've told you enough for one day."

"Anything from India?"

Malone sat up straight in his chair. "Yeah, the last one. I got it a month ago. Just what the hell —"

The phone shrieked into the silent room. Both Malone and Helen jerked in their chairs. Malone glanced at Helen, then picked up the receiver and growled a greeting. Helen watched with growing interest as his eyes widened, and his mouth formed the name Bennett.

"Well, I'm glad you've been reading my work. I always — no, no. I wouldn't say that. I've only asked what the public has a right to know." A few moments of nods and murmurs followed. "Yes, that would be very convenient. At your house, you say?" He scribbled on a notepad. Helen didn't bother to hide her interest, but his writing was illegible. "Fine, fine, Mr. Bennett. I'd be glad to hear anything you

have to say in response. All right, sir. Yes. Goodbye."
Malone hung up, a grin spreading over his face. "I
gather you figured out the gist of that little
conversation."

"You're meeting Bennett this afternoon."

"Finally. Finally I get to rake the little bastard
over the proverbial coals. Roast his lily-white ass."
His eyes shone and he looked joyous at the prospect.

"Must be because of the press conference."

"Why else? God, this is going to be good. I didn't
know I'd shaken him up so much."

"Look, Malone, I don't buy it. Why the hell
should you have it in for Bennett? So you loved Liz,
and she didn't get along with her family. Big deal.
You should hear me on the subject of my family.
Why are you targeting Bob Bennett?"

Malone looked at her as if he couldn't believe she
was that stupid. "As far as I'm concerned, Big Bob
Bennett killed Liz just as sure as if he'd driven a
stake through her heart. You didn't know her. I did.
That woman was afraid of nothing and no one. Hell,
she traveled alone around the world, she took on the
ugliest sons of bitches you care to meet, nothing
stopped her. But that day, when she saw the article
on Bennett, she was a wreck. You saw how he
waffled around when I asked him about her death at
the press conference. Who else could have talked the
police into dropping the case that fast? Who else had
that kind of muscle? It sure ain't me. Or you." His
face went bright red with anger as he finished his
speech, and Helen silently watched him rein in his
fury. "What the hell. I don't really expect you to
understand any of this."

"Maybe I understand better than you think I do. That still doesn't change the situation, does it?"

"What situation?" he asked, tired now.

"The fact that I've got your notebook, and what you've told me just doesn't add up. There's still no reason to suspect Bennett knew a single thing about her death."

Malone sighed, rolled his eyes. "Good God, woman, just tell me what else you want. I need those notes!"

Helen considered, already sure of what she wanted to do, but wanting Malone to sweat a few seconds longer. "I'll give them back to you this afternoon." She smiled at his obvious relief, then added, "After you and I go together to Bennett's house for the interview."

"No way, bitch."

"Fine, Malone. No way? No notebook." It didn't take long to convince him she meant business. As he cursed and scowled, Helen agreed to meet him at one-thirty at her office on Shattuck. "I mean it, Malone. If you don't show up I'll shred the whole thing and put it in my cat's litter box."

"Why not? In the last couple of days I've been run over, hung out to dry, and now I'll get shit on. Sounds like the story of my life." She left him there, sitting in the stuffy office like a disheveled Buddha waiting for a peace that would never come.

Chapter Thirteen

The route from the auto repair shop back to Helen's office took her directly past the Darcy Building. The clock at the university tolled ten times — still a few hours to go until she and Malone were due to visit the Bennett household. After a moment's indecision she turned her car into a side street and parked. Maybe, she thought, there was something in the deserted building the police had missed, something that hadn't caught her attention when she and Cecily went there yesterday.

Helen found an empty parking space after about

five minutes of driving. Another five minutes' walk brought her back to the building where Liz had been found. Its crumbled facade etched a ragged seam against the bright blue spring sky. The usual shuffling mob of homeless sat in clumps of four or five in the scruffy grass across the street, and Helen could see, in the distance, a handful of people carrying picket signs that displayed a variety of opinions about the closing of People's Park.

With one hand firmly holding her flashlight, the other clutching her car keys, Helen strode past the small crowd and up to the entrance of the Darcy Building. She paused and listened. Only faint scrabblings could be heard from the interior, the sort of sounds made by plaster and dust as it shifted and settled. Helen took one careful step into the gloom, edging against the wall, and waited for her eyes to adjust.

The boy saw her first. He dropped something as he cried out. Whatever it was hit the floor with a soft plop and dissolved in a shapeless heap. In the narrow strip of light Helen saw his glasses flash as he darted forward, trying to get past her out into the street. Some low-placed obstacle tripped up his gangly legs and sent him crashing to the ground.

Helen swiftly picked her way through the debris toward him. He was howling in pain, and for a few seconds she wasn't sure if he had done himself some real damage. Her grasp on his arm stopped the screaming. Something about the way she touched him seemed to bring reassurance, and he stammered, "I'm okay, I'm okay. Just leave me alone."

"The hell with that," Helen responded. "What on earth are you doing here?" He struggled briefly to get free, turning his face into view. "Wait a minute. I've seen you before."

"No, I don't think so. I never —"

"Yes, it was last night. You were hanging around the alley in back of the Clarion! Right? I said, right?"

"Ow! Let go, that hurts!" He rubbed his arm when she dropped it. Looking at her through his thick lenses he said, "So what? Is that a crime or something?"

The glasses sitting askew on his long, thin nose made him look so comical that Helen nearly laughed aloud. "It's no crime, but it's certainly strange." She stood up and regarded him. "Shouldn't you be in school?"

He ignored her question. "Maybe I should ask what you were doing at the Clarion last night," he said with false bluster.

Helen moved between him and the doorway. "I was with the police," she said calmly. It was half true, anyway.

He stood up so quickly that his glasses fell onto the floor. "Don't get excited," she said. "I'm not a cop, I'm a private investigator."

"No shit!" As he shoved the glasses back on, he looked at her with more interest than fear. "You mean, you're on a case? About that Bennett woman?"

Helen, instead of answering him, played her flashlight around the empty room until its light rested on the object he'd been carrying when she entered the building. She grabbed it before he had a chance to stop her. When he saw he didn't have much chance to get it away from her he tried once again to escape.

But Helen grabbed his arm and flung him up against the wall. She was a whole lot bigger than he was, and the boy looked terrified. "All right, who are you?"

He was too upset to protest. "Martin. Martin Pfister," he blurted.

"Martin, what are you doing in here?" Helen lifted the bag with her free hand. "And what is this?"

"Just let me go," he whined. Helen looked at him with mixed feelings of pity, anger and disgust as he wiped his nose and eyes, his pitted face screwed up in an agony of fear and shame. "I didn't do anything wrong. I was just trying to put it back."

"Put it back? Meaning you took it from here?" She loosened her hold a bit but stood too close for him to get away.

He winced and tried without success to squirm out of her grasp. "I don't know what made me take it. It was just lying there in the room next to — to her. The cops thought it was my school books." In spite of his fright he managed to sound proud of putting one over on the authorities. Then the moment of courage faded and he became a piteous child again. "My folks will kill me if they find out about this."

Realization dawned. "You discovered the body. And you found this with it."

"I didn't do anything wrong," he repeated. "She was just a tramp, I thought. Nobody. I didn't even think it was her stuff." This time he writhed free of her hand. "I was just putting it back. Honest. I didn't keep anything. Really I didn't!" He fled.

Helen let out a muttered curse, grabbed the bag

and took off after him. Since Frieda had left her she'd taken to slothlike behavior. Now the months of relative inactivity tugged at her muscles, and when she reached Martin she was sweating and out of breath. Aware of the spectacle they were presenting to the ragtag crowd that had collected on the street, she pulled her prey back onto the sidewalk. Panting she marched him to her car.

"We're not finished, buddy," she gasped as she shoved him into the passenger seat and slammed the door shut. He slumped next to her as she got in beside him. "I want it all or we drive to the police right now."

He was apparently too upset to demand she let him go or even to think of getting out and running off, which would have been the easiest solution. Instead, he seemed glad to finally have a chance to pour out the whole story, to let a responsible adult take care of things. He spilled it all out in one incoherent burst — how he and his two friends had wandered into the building in search of drugs or stolen articles or whatever else they could rustle up. How he'd gone off by himself and inspected the building. How he'd stumbled right over some huge lump that turned into a fast-decaying corpse.

When he got to the part about taking off on his own search, Helen suspected he was concealing something. His blush and stammer gave it away, but he turned defiant eyes toward her. "It's the truth. That's what happened."

"All right. Then what?"

"Then nothing," he answered, sullen. "I ran out of there and called the cops, that's what. Look, if you don't believe me you can call them." His belligerence was making a belated appearance, spurred on by the relief he must have felt at unburdening his troubles to Helen.

"You left something out."

"What?" She held out the bag between them and his face fell. "Oh. That."

"Yeah. That." She shook it and he looked out of the window. "Why did you take this? Didn't you realize it might be evidence?"

He sighed and leaned his head back against the seat. "I was going to tell Hallie and Jeremy about it, you know? I thought they might respect me more, make me more like part of the crowd. Besides, I thought there might be some good stuff in it." He glanced at her, then looked away again.

Helen was silent, remembering her own youth, remembering what it felt like never to belong, to be the object of ridicule no matter what one did. When she finally spoke it was in a gentler voice. "You know the police have to have this. You know that, don't you?"

"You can take it, can't you? You were with them the other night, you said. Can't you take it and not say anything about me? Pretend like you just found it yourself?" He was already starting to get out of her car, pleased at having hit on such an easy solution.

"Relax. I can't run anymore this morning. Leave this with me." She sighed, fishing in the glove compartment for one of her cards. "I'll figure something out."

He took the card and turned it over in both hands, inspecting front and back. "You — you won't tell my parents, will you? I mean, they were pretty upset about the body and all. They don't have to know about this, do they?"

Helen drummed her fingers on the steering wheel as she thought. The police had already dropped the whole thing. She'd let Manny know about this and have him take a look at it. Besides, they'd know how to get in touch with this kid if they needed to. "I'm not going to tell them. The police may want to know more from you, though. I don't have any control over that."

He leaned his head forward in his hands and moaned. "There's nothing in there, nothing! Just some old clothes and junk, a couple of photographs! Shit, I knew this was going to be awful."

Helen quickly rummaged through the contents of the bag. Just as Martin said, it didn't seem to amount to much. With a sigh she placed it on the floor behind the driver's seat. "Quit crying, Martin. I doubt that the police will bother you anymore."

Uncertainly Martin opened the passenger door and set one foot on the ground. Seeing that Helen wasn't going to stop him, he slipped out of the car. "Are you sure?" he asked one last time.

"I'll take care of everything. Trust me."

He slammed the door shut. Through the half-open window Helen heard him say, "Yeah. Trust me. Where have I heard that one before?"

Chapter Fourteen

Helen found her mind wandering as Robert Bennett droned on to Malone. They'd been sitting in Bennett's study for nearly half an hour — Helen in complete silence, Malone growling out a series of meaningless questions about Bennett's work. Apparently no one questioned Helen's right to be present in the capacity of Malone's "assistant," although Helen grimaced inwardly at the title. She had a ludicrous vision of Clark Kent squiring Lois Lane, with Jimmy Olsen waiting eagerly in the wings.

She pretended to take notes, while her eyes and ears took in as much as possible. Lydia Bennett, the matriarch of the family, had received them at the door with a sour expression. Beyond a brief bark of greeting she hadn't spoken once. Helen was surprised when she took her place standing next to her son, who was seated grandly at a huge oak desk. Neither of Bennett's daughters was anywhere in sight, for which Helen was grateful.

The study itself was immense — a lesson in perfection. The carpet was so freshly cleaned that Helen and Malone had left indentations in its gray plush when they entered the room and were waved to chairs. Everything shone with the dull gleam of understated wealth. Helen sank down into a deep leather armchair and looked across the expanse of oak into the handsome face of Bob Bennett. A pristine white blotter was the only object on the desk. Bennett was toying with a slim gold pen until he set it down on the blotter to shake hands first with Malone, then with Helen.

Malone had begun innocently enough by talking about Project Nightlight. Of course, Bennett was only too happy to expound, although Lydia eyeballed Malone and Helen warily. One claw rested on her son's shoulder, giving him a sober reminder of her presence as he spoke.

Helen studied his even, handsome features — the thick auburn hair that brushed against his collar each time he moved his head, the smile that spread with crooked charm over his perfect teeth, the square jaw he jutted with purpose and conviction each time he made a point. From time to time he glanced Helen's way, as if not quite sure what to make of her, but Malone skillfully kept the questions coming.

"So you think Project Nightlight will go nationwide soon?" Malone was asking.

"Sure do!" Bennett reached up to pat his mother's hand, which still lay on his shoulder. "With my family standing behind me, I can do it. The governor's convinced we can start a whole new way of dealing with the problem of child abuse in this country."

"Just the other day we got a call from the mayor of New York!" Alice bubbled. She had been sitting so quietly near the back of the room that everyone turned around, startled, to be reminded of her presence. "He wants Bob to come and talk to various community organizations about setting up a similar project there." Alice left her chair and came closer to the desk. She stood next to Lydia, beaming her adoring eyes on her husband. Helen saw the way Lydia flinched when Alice brushed against her, although the elderly woman hid it fairly well.

Lydia sighed. "Perhaps these representatives of the press would like some coffee, Alice?" The hint was taken and Alice left them with a smile.

Lydia sighed again and slowly hobbled to a low chair near Helen. Instinctively Helen reached out a hand to help her but Lydia ignored it. "Thank God. Now we can really talk," she said. With stiff movements she adjusted herself until she faced Malone. "I don't know what you think you're up to, but it won't do you or this girl Friday of yours any good."

Malone raised his eyebrows. Bennett squirmed in his chair and began once again to roll his gold pen back and forth, from palm to palm. "Now, Mother, that's going a little too far —"

"You can see, my dears," Lydia rasped, "that I brought up my only son to be very polite. What Robert doesn't understand, of course, is that this little interview is a bit — shall we say — premature?"

Malone was quietly deferential, but Helen could see his eyes flashing. "I'm afraid I don't understand what you mean, Mrs. Bennett."

Bennett laughed, uncertain. "I'm afraid my mother usually organizes my press interviews. It's too bad I wasn't able to tell her about this ahead of time."

Lydia ignored her son and spoke directly to Malone, her eyes now and then drifting toward Helen. "I suppose that the name Jim Leslie means something to you? I see by that pained expression that it does. Well, Jim Leslie may be a rather difficult man from time to time, but he does sign your paychecks, doesn't he? I should let you know right now that I've already arranged to have the final say on how this meeting appears in your paper." She leaned back in her chair with a satisfied smile. "Now that that's been made clear, I think we can agree that my son has explained the purposes of the project fully. In fact, there's nothing left to say."

Malone paled, then blushed as Lydia spoke. "We'll see about that, Mrs. Bennett. There are other cities, other newspapers, that might want to know what kind of a man your son is — what kind of a family this is. They might," he said, his voice rising in anger, "want the taxpayers to know that their dollars are supporting worthless jackasses like Bob Bennett."

"That will do, Mr. Malone." Lydia's green eyes closed and her voice froze over. "You may have gotten away with that kind of behavior at the press conference, but you will not act this way in my house. Kindly take your assistant and go."

"Your house, huh?" Malone turned to eye Bennett, who slumped miserably in his chair. "This used to be home to Liz, once upon a time. Isn't that right, Bennett?" He grabbed the edge of the desk with his huge paws, leaning over until his face was inches away from Bennett, who flinched.

"I'm not leaving until you tell me about Liz." Malone spoke directly to Bennett. The man glanced uneasily at his mother. Helen had no doubt that Malone had entirely forgotten her presence. Bennett rose from his chair at last and rounded the desk, the gold pen dropping to the floor where it rolled under the desk. "It's all your fault she died, you old hag," Malone muttered, turning his glare on Lydia. "You all killed her. All of you."

Bennett stepped in front of his mother. "All right, Malone." His voice boomed. He gloried in his moment of manly strength as he pitted his own height against the reporter's. "I think you'd better leave now."

"Oh, stop fussing, Robert! Our guests are just leaving." With a cruel gleam in her eyes, a smile playing about her thin lips, Lydia watched Malone back away. "I don't think we have anything to be afraid of from them."

Malone was in such a hurry to get out of the

house that they nearly barreled over Alice, who had emerged from the kitchen with a coffee tray just as they were bounding down the hallway to the front door. She gave a faint cry of fright as Malone pushed his way out from the dark foyer into the midday sunlight. Helen had to break into a trot to keep up with him. She knew he'd much rather that she disappear than witness his humiliation.

They didn't stop until they'd reached Malone's car. Helen opened her shoulder bag as they turned onto Telegraph and headed back to her office. "Here's your notebook, Frank."

He took it from her with a grunt. "Thought it was hidden away in your office."

"I lied."

He couldn't help laughing. "Maybe you'd make a decent reporter after all." Then his face fell. "How the fuck should I know what makes a good reporter? Can't even stand up to an old bitch like Lydia Bennett. She's right. Leslie could make my life a living hell." One meaty hand rubbed his forehead as he sighed. Helen stayed quiet, unable to think of anything reassuring to say.

The car lurched forward, threatened to stall, then sailed on in a sudden burst of acceleration. "Goddam rented cars."

"Is your car totaled?"

He grimaced and turned onto Shattuck. "Not quite. On my salary, and with my insurance, I'll have to fix her up and make her do."

The car stopped in front of her office building. As Helen opened the door she said, "It's not over yet, Malone. I'm not quitting. I think you're right. The Bennetts definitely know something about all this."

As she spoke, she found herself wondering if she really believed her own words.

"Yeah, well, right now we're holding up traffic. Thanks for the notebook."

He raced off in a whirl of exhaust, the blare of horns echoing behind him. Helen knew her last remark had been the wrong thing to say, but there probably hadn't been any right thing to say.

She turned and went up the steps into her office. Helen was not surprised to find the air stale and thick with heat trapped from the last couple of days. She walked quickly to the windows and threw them open. Fresh air rushed in, cooling her face and piercing her thin sweater. Across the room, loose pages ruffled on her desk. They floated slightly, reminding her of Bennett's immaculate study. The contrast was almost funny, and she had a brief flash of the blotter, a white drift on a sea of oak.

The backpack still lay locked in the office safe where she'd put it before Malone showed up. She slung it over one shoulder and, after closing up the windows against the spring, headed back down to the street and her meeting with Manny.

Chapter Fifteen

Manny's house was situated at the end of a scruffy cul-de-sac off Martin Luther King Boulevard. Across the street a group of kids played a noisy game of basketball on a dilapidated court. An ice cream truck made a stately procession down the street, accompanied by an uneven train of children drawn to its tinkling music. Helen was greeted at the front door by the master of the house. He handed her a glass as soon as she set the backpack on the dining room table.

"Don't worry, it's just iced tea. I haven't picked up any bad habits since you left me."

Helen drank half the glass immediately, surprised at her own thirst. "Thanks."

"More?"

"That would be great." She sat down as Manny disappeared into the kitchen. Above her, rap music boomed through the ceiling — one of Manny's kids.

"That's John," Manny said, emerging with her refilled glass. He loped up the stairs and Helen heard him pounding his son's door. Shortly thereafter the decibel level diminished noticeably. "Sorry about that." Manny grinned. "My old man would die to hear me telling my kids to turn down the music!"

He sat down and listened while Helen told him of her meeting with Martin Pfister. "You're sure this belongs to Elizabeth Bennett?" he asked as she handed him the bag.

"Go ahead, take a look." Manny unzipped the backpack and emptied its contents onto the formica table top. It was a meager collection, almost pathetic — one worn but clean pair of jeans; a couple of T-shirts bearing logos of long-forgotten events and places; socks and underthings that had seen better days. One interesting item was a small silk jewelry bag of Oriental design. Helen watched Manny finger its handmade elegance.

"This doesn't quite fit," he murmured. Carefully he unrolled it, and two items were exposed. "Shit," he breathed, looking down at the fine gold chain and the black-and-white photograph. It was unmistakably a Bennett family portrait. Several years old, it showed a younger and happier Lydia standing behind a pyramid of her descendants. Her son and his wife sat at Lydia's right, looking like Ken and Barbie. Bob sported the long sideburns popular in the early seventies, while Alice, her blonde shag cascading over her shoulders, held a baby against her breast. Jane, the older daughter, stood sullenly next to her father, her heavy features already weighed down with bitterness.

On Lydia's left sat a young woman who looked startlingly like Cecily. She stared without smiling into the camera, but her sober expression was neither angry nor sullen. She looked into the lens with a calm resignation, as if this group portrait were one trial among many to be borne. Her body faced slightly away from the rest of the family, setting up a thin but tangible barrier between them and herself. The glimmer of a thin gold chain — the only adornment she wore — circled her slender neck. The overall impression she gave was one of austerity, accentuated by the plain dark blouse and the light-colored hair pulled straight back from a face bereft of any makeup.

Helen got up and stood next to Manny, leaning over him to gaze at the photograph again. "That's got to be her," he said. "I know twenty years have gone by, and the poor woman is dead, but that's her."

With a sigh he set down the photograph, moved the silk bag to one side, and sorted through the clothes. A few other items fell out. A hairbrush with a broken handle stuck out of a pocket in the jeans. He began to get excited when he found a small spiral notebook, but deflated again when a quick study showed nothing but empty white pages. A thin gold mechanical pencil rolled out from the last pile of clothes, and Manny clipped it onto the notebook, then leaned back in his chair.

"This doesn't seem to tell us very much, Helen," he said glumly. "Nothing to indicate where she'd come from, or how long she'd been back in the States. No plane tickets, no addresses, no ID, no letters — just this photograph." He reached for the notebook and flipped through it. "Maybe there was something in here, but the pages could have been ripped out long ago."

"Hey, don't get mad at me. I just thought something here might jog in your mind with stuff you'd already found during the investigation."

Manny snorted in scorn. "Shit, there was no investigation! Like I said the other night. We got a call from the commissioner — the commissioner himself — after only a couple of days. He called me and Mike and Lieutenant Harris into his office for a little meeting."

Helen sat down again. "Well, what happened?"

"Oh, he told us what a fine job we'd done so far, and it was clearly just a case of transients killing each other off." He drummed his fingers on the table, picking up the beat of the music thudding over their heads. "Some homicidal homeless maniac stabs her in the back one night for whatever goodies she might have in her pockets. Who knows? Maybe he's right."

"What about the knife?"

He shook his head. "We didn't have time to find out where it came from. Definitely not U.S. made. It reminded Mike of some of the stuff he'd seen in Vietnam — knives used by, as he put it so charmingly, 'gooks.' "

"That would fit," Helen mused. "If she'd spent time in India, or Indochina. Maybe the knife was hers?"

"No clear prints on it. It might have been."

"Okay. What about the family? Where were they the night she was killed?"

"No good, Helen. Last Tuesday night everyone was at some big party for the governor. In fact, Bennett was one of several speakers that night, so he was seen by a lot of people. And before you ask, I may as well tell you Mike and I were definitely warned away from questioning these people. We're talking governor's office, a U.S. senator, and a huge pile of money." Grimacing, he set his glass down with a thud. "It makes me want to puke. I have never seen such ass-licking as I have the past couple of weeks."

Helen sighed and closed her eyes against the headache that was forming like a firm grip across her scalp. "Tell me what you think, Manny. What's your gut feeling about all this?"

He shrugged, reached out and fingered the pile of clothes absently. "It's quite possible she was just in the wrong place at the wrong time. Maybe she wandered in there when something else was going down, a drug deal, whatever."

"Why would she wander in there in the first place? It doesn't wash. Christ." She rubbed her hand over her brow.

"What is it? Headache?"

"Yeah. Too much fun lately."

"You want some aspirin?" Manny offered, half-rising from his seat.

"No, no, I'll be okay," Helen protested. "Listen, why don't you take this stuff in for me? You could put it quietly in the evidence room, just keep it there with the knife for a while."

"Sure. Next thing I know it'll disappear. Believe me, Helen, no one at the station wants to be reminded of Elizabeth Bennett." He zipped the bag with a rough gesture. "I was going to go to the funeral tomorrow, but the big guys are keeping Mike and me so busy we can't even take a dump without getting written permission."

Helen sat up, alert again, the pain in her head diminished. "It's tomorrow?"

"Yeah, at St. Monica's." A smile cracked across his face. "How 'bout it, Sherlock? Want to pay our respects tomorrow morning at ten o'clock?"

"Not a bad idea. I'll try to lurk in the background and be inconspicuous, like all the other ghouls." She slung her purse over her shoulder. "Thanks, Manny."

Manny stood still, watching her. "Are you sure you're okay, Helen?"

"I'm fine. Why?"

"Nothing, really. Have you — ah — heard from Frieda again?"

Helen had to smile at his awkward blushing. Nothing had changed. He still felt uncomfortable referring to the relationship between the two women. "Not for a few hours. Does it show that much?"

"I'm not sure. You just look different, or

something. Hell, I don't know. Look, this is not easy for me to say, but I know things have been tough for you without her."

Helen didn't respond. Manny followed her to the door. John switched tapes to heavy metal. Manny groaned. "I guess the new music system was better than the set of drums he really wanted for his birthday. Helen, I'm just trying to say that I'm worried about you."

The headache sharpened. "I can take care of myself."

"Don't you think I know that?" He sighed in exasperation. "Did you ever think maybe I miss having you around? Don't be such a fucking hermit, all right?" He covered his emotion by pushing her toward her car. "Try to stay out of trouble." He went back into the house, slamming the door after him.

Helen wearily started the engine and drove it in a numb daze the few blocks to her home. Boobella whined at her feet, almost tripping her up, and she put a small heap of dry cat food into a bowl in the kitchen before dragging herself into the bedroom. Why the hell was she so tired? Before she could answer her own question she had fallen asleep.

Chapter Sixteen

Like all dreams, this one followed its own
internal logic and refused to offer clear explanation.
It started with Helen wandering aimlessly through
the Bennett household. The long dark hallway had
somehow become even longer and darker, lined with
heavy wooden panels instead of the family portraits
and pictures Helen had noted earlier that day. Her
steps echoed ominously, as though her shoes were
ringed with iron. Door after door refused to yield to
her search. After what seemed an eternity, she
entered a room at the end of the hall.

It was Bennett's study. Helen knew, rather than felt, that the room was icy. Curtains billowed like sails in a biting wind, blasts of winter air filled the room, howling, shrieking. She looked around her, confused, but operating on the suspension of disbelief that all dreams demand. She accepted that the room was now empty of all furniture except for the huge oak desk. As she approached the desk, she looked down at the floor. It was carpeted, but her steps still clattered. Her shoes left huge indentations on the pile, as though each step carried enormous weight. Each movement in the cavernous room was slow, as if waterlogged. Bursts of wind threatened to push her over, but she persisted until she'd reached the desk.

But it wasn't Bob Bennett who sat crouched over some piece of writing beneath the bright white light. It was a woman, her face hidden by long fair hair that fell in smooth bands over her features. A simple black sheath covered the slender body. Helen stood for some time, watching the pale hands scribbling in the small notebook.

A stab of recognition pierced Helen. It was the spiral notebook from the backpack she'd taken from Martin Pfister. And the pencil sweeping over the clean sheets — surely that was the same one found among Liz Bennett's paltry earthly belongings, wasn't it? Its gold surface winked in the light as it moved back and forth. The only sound in the room was of its harsh scratches on the pages of the notebook.

Finally the stooped figure looked up. Elizabeth Bennett's spare face looked into Helen's, the eyes glazed and unseeing. Helen recoiled from the dull, dead stare, the stare of nonexistence she'd confronted too many times. She tried to back away from the ghostly presence, but her body seemed rooted to the floor, preventing escape. Liz stood up slowly in a single silent movement. The thin pale lips opened in speech, but all Helen heard was gibberish, babbled out in a monotone, without inflection or cadence — the dead words of a madwoman. Helen panicked as the woman moved closer, gliding soundlessly across the thick carpet. The cacophonous speech ended. Now she thrust the notebook at her, but the writing she saw might have been hieroglyphs. Then the pencil was shoved under her nose by a shaking white hand, pushed forward again and again, urging her to — what? Look at it? Write something with it? Take it away?

"What do you want?" Helen tried to say. The words faded before they left her lips, leaving only a faint murmur behind. Frustrated, increasingly upset, Helen struggled mightily against the spell of the dream and fought her way through to consciousness.

"Hello," a soft voice said as Helen opened her eyes. For the first few seconds Helen thought she was still staring into the cold dead eyes of Liz Bennett. Then the rest of the room focused. The bright white light became her bedside lamp, the wind blowing through the study thinned into the mutter of traffic outside. The notebook fluttered into nothingness. Then the features that had, moments ago, been frozen and lifeless, took on a more familiar cast.

"Cecily! What the hell are you doing here?" Helen cried out as she sprang up, her heart pounding.

Cecily backed off, her hands held up in surrender. "Hey, take it easy. I'm sorry."

111

Still shaking and angry, Helen didn't let her get any further. "What are you doing in my house? How did you get in?" Helen took a few paces around the room to quiet her nerves, checking surreptitiously to make sure she was still fully clothed. Thank God she'd just tumbled onto the bed without bothering to undress.

Cecily stood, watching her from the middle of the room. "Your door was wide open when I got here. I called for you, but you didn't answer. Don't be mad — I was worried something was wrong when I saw the door and all the lights on."

Helen sighed and sank into a chair. "Okay. Sorry. You gave me quite a shock. I guess I forgot to lock the door when I came in."

"Look, you can't get mad at me. I rescued your cat." Boobella made a noisy appearance into the bedroom. She leapt nimbly up into Cecily's arms, as if they were old friends. "The cat was crying in the driveway when I got here. This is Boobella, right?"

Helen nodded, about to ask her how she'd known the cat's name, then realized that Frieda must have told her. With a spasm of uneasiness, she wondered what else Frieda might have revealed. She was trying to figure out a way to get Cecily out of the bedroom when the girl sat down on her rumpled bed.

"Why are you here, Cecily?"

Cecily ruffled the cat's thick black fur, eliciting a rumbling purr of intense pleasure. She turned away from Helen's stare. "The funeral is tomorrow," she said, refusing to answer Helen's question directly. "Frieda didn't think she should go."

"St. Monica's. Ten o'clock."

"You're going to be there?"

Helen rubbed the sleep from her eyes and said, "Well, I figured I'd hang out with Malone and the other members of the press and see what I could see."

Cecily nodded. "It's old news now. There won't be a big crowd. Just the family, all turned out to see that she gets decently buried."

She put the cat down on the bed and lay down on her side, turning so that she faced Helen. "Are you okay now?" she asked. "You must have been having a nightmare. You were tossing and mumbling when I found you."

"Great," Helen muttered, getting up from her chair. "That must have been quite a lovely sight."

"Actually, it was." Cecily raised up on one elbow and regarded Helen with an air of amusement. "You looked very pretty."

Helen laughed aloud at the remark. "Yeah, right."

"Why are you in such a hurry to get out of the bedroom?" Cecily lay flat and watched Helen prowl. "Does my being here make you uncomfortable?"

"For God's sake, Cecily. Do you want to hear me fawning over you, is that it? Fine. You're a good-looking woman. Okay? Satisfied?" Even as she said the words Helen knew her anger was just adding fuel to the sparks.

Cecily smiled and slid lazily off the bed. "I already know Frieda was here last night. It's okay. We don't hide anything from each other."

"Well, maybe you should." Helen ran her hands through her hair, trying to get a grip on the confusion of feelings that raced through her. "Don't you feel *anything* for your aunt, Cecily? She's going

113

to be buried tomorrow. This is no time to be acting like a spoiled brat." Helen leaned against the doorframe and shook her head. "I can't figure you out at all. Why don't you just tell me what you want and then get out of here?"

Helen was totally unprepared when Cecily moved close to her, then suddenly leaned closer and brushed her lips on Helen's. The pressure of her mouth, her body, was so unexpectedly gentle that Helen was taken by surprise. She hardly knew how it was that her own mouth responded, yielding and resisting at once.

Their tongues met shyly, hesitantly. Cecily's hands felt their way to her hair, and her body trembled as Helen put her arms around her. Helen felt a strange sensation, as if she were watching all this from a great distance. Maybe it was the effect of being awakened so suddenly from a strange dream — maybe it was her exhaustion — but Helen felt as if she were acting a part, playing a role in someone else's script. But the feeling didn't prevent her from enjoying the kiss, the sensation of Cecily's hands moving slowly under her shirt over her back. It had been years since Helen had touched anyone besides Frieda, and the memory of Frieda's visit the night before was still fresh in her mind. Cecily was small, like Frieda, but her body was softer, rounder.

Helen finally broke free. "Look, Cecily, this is crazy."

"Yeah, I know," Cecily whispered, tracing her fingers across Helen's neck. "But it feels good, doesn't it?"

"Stop." Helen took Cecily's arms and pushed them away. "This is getting us nowhere. I mean it." She

114

forced a hard edge into her voice. Once Cecily finally let go, Helen strode down the hallway toward the kitchen. Cecily followed, a smile around her lips. "I want to know what you're doing here."

"Besides trying to seduce you? I just wanted to find out what happened this afternoon when you and that reporter came to see Dad." Cecily leaned against the counter and watched Helen poke around the kitchen.

"Nothing happened," Helen answered, abrupt and angry. She fumbled with the coffeepot and managed to spill half the grounds into the sink before successfully getting the pot onto the stove. "We just pissed your grandmother off."

Cecily laughed, her bright voice shattering the kitchen like broken glass. Helen's head started to hurt again. "Don't pay any attention to Grandma. Everything pisses her off. Me, most of all, I think."

"Don't you think you ought to be with your family right now, Cecily?" Helen found some cold cuts that appeared edible, then started a search for the bread.

"I'm leaving soon. I really came to tell you about a plan I thought up today."

Shit. No mayonnaise. Helen choked down a bite of her dry sandwich. "What plan is that?" she finally asked.

Cecily picked up a piece of baloney and nibbled at it. "How would you like to get back into my father's office tomorrow?"

Helen chewed and tried to keep her face from showing her interest. "Fat chance."

"But tomorrow's the perfect time. There's going to be a kind of reception held in the hall at St.

Monica's after — after the burial," Cecily said, faltering a little over her words. "The governor will be there, so Daddy and Grandma will stay. The house ought to be empty."

Helen laid her sandwich down. Boobella emerged from the dark corridor and mewed, sniffing the air at the scent of baloney. "Are you certain, Cecily? I can't afford to have you fuck this one up."

Cecily finished the meat and stood behind Helen, her fingers tracing the nape of Helen's neck. "Hey, would I lie to you?"

Helen laughed and jerked away. "Of course you would. But that's a risk I'm willing to take. For a few hours tomorrow, anyway."

"Life is full of risks, Helen." Cecily's hands left her neck and Helen watched her walk to the door. "Just go to my house right after the ceremony and I'll meet you outside." With a final stroke given to the cat, Cecily disappeared.

Helen waited until she heard the front door close before she got up and poured herself a cup of coffee. Boobella continued to complain in piercing cries. "I know," Helen said, giving the cat the remainder of the sandwich. "I don't like this setup, either."

Chapter Seventeen

As the clouds gathered overhead Helen cursed herself for not bringing her umbrella to the cemetery. No one ever expected these late May showers, especially since they'd had several days of constant warm sunshine. A few stray drops pelted the withering bouquets that adorned the surrounding graves. Stone angels bowed in unending vigil beneath the increasing gloom. Helen pulled her jacket tighter against the sudden cold wind. The skirt of the dark blue suit — the same one she'd worn to the Clarion — shifted loosely around her waist. She'd definitely lost some weight in the last year, having lost her appetite about the same time she'd lost Frieda.

Another gust of wind blew a few more drops into her eyes. Helen decided to edge a bit closer to the funeral party. She saw a handful of people hovering like herself in the distance. Probably reporters hoping to milk the story for all it was worth. They hunched against the cold, their faces revealing their boredom and irritation. The funeral would probably be good for a few lines hidden away on an obscure page of tomorrow's paper. They wouldn't even have been here unless Bob Bennett had figured in the story. Helen had seen Malone earlier, in the church, but decided to stay away from him. She'd seen his car chuffing off down the street as she'd followed the others out of the building. Maybe the sight of his former lover's remains being put into the ground had been too much for him, especially when faced with confronting the rest of the Bennett clan.

They'd made a rather poor showing today. Only the immediate family was there, supported by a small entourage of people from the governor's office. Lydia's face had frozen in ill-concealed rage when she'd first surveyed the official entourage. The governor himself was nowhere to be seen. Clearly affronted by his absence, Lydia had acknowledged these emissaries with a hauteur bordering on rudeness. Of course, they would gloss over her behavior by ascribing it to grief.

And who was to say, Helen mused, watching Lydia lean on her son's arm at the gravesite, that it wasn't grief? Helen's brief encounter with Lydia in Bennett's office had revealed only her powerful personality. Stoicism at a funeral didn't mean lack of sorrow.

The small gathering next to the coffin — closed, at the family's request — listened to the dulcet tones of the priest. Recalling the frenzied outbursts of her own Pentecostal youth, Helen was mesmerized by the quiet cadences of the Anglican service. The priest, a very young man who might only yesterday have graduated from divinity school, was obviously doing his best to give a sense of dignity to the burial of a woman he'd never known. The ritual itself served the purpose of creating a calm, if mournful, atmosphere. Helen spotted Cecily looking at her. She was standing behind Alice with a stricken look on her face. Helen still didn't fully understand the mixed emotions Cecily held toward Liz. That early sense of rejection Cecily said she'd felt as a child, when her beloved aunt had disappeared forever, seemed mingled with guilt over her refusal to meet with Liz at the hotel. Who knew if Liz Bennett's death might have been prevented by Cecily's response to the letter?

The cluster of people shifted as Bob Bennett was handed a small spade. He bent to the small heap of earth before him, lifted the shovel with its burden of dirt, and let the soil fall with a soft plop onto the casket. The sound wasn't loud enough to cover Cecily's sobs. Bennett next handed the tool to Lydia. Helen watched as the aging matriarch, assisted by her son, tossed a clod or two down. Was it really carelessness Helen saw in the gesture, or just the weak physical efforts of an elderly woman afflicted with arthritis?

Alice was next, then Jane, then Cecily. By now

Cecily had her tears under control. The young priest took a step nearer to her, perhaps moved by the fact that she was the only person in the group showing any signs of real grief. After she had thrown dirt on the coffin, she stood uncertainly, staring white-faced down into the grave. She clutched the spade as if unwilling to end this final act of connection with the dead woman. Finally the priest took it away and placed it back on the mound of earth.

With that gesture it was over. The funeral party began to walk away from the gravesite, heading back to the church. Cecily broke away from the rest of her family and walked quickly, almost running, through the stone monuments. Helen followed at a respectable distance, noting the way the rest of the family seemed to draw away from one another. Lydia walked much slower than the rest, falling behind the group. Helen watched as Alice reached out a hand to Lydia's elbow only to have it brushed aside with a violent gesture. Alice froze for a moment, then trudged ahead, leaving her husband to make the procession through the wet grass to the church.

Helen waited until they were all inside before heading back out to the street. The rain was coming down hard now, and she had already climbed hurriedly into her car before she saw another familiar car sitting on the other side of the street. Helen groaned. What did Frieda think she was doing? There was no mistaking the car, or the woman sitting in the driver's seat. Frieda waved a hand in greeting. Helen closed her eyes and leaned back in the seat, sick to death of all the conflicting emotions this case produced.

The next thing she knew Frieda was tapping on

the window, her eyes squinting against the rain. Resigned, Helen unlocked the door and Frieda slid into the passenger seat.

If Frieda was expecting a joyous reception, she wasn't going to get it. "I don't know what you think you're doing here," Helen snapped. "It's not —"

"Hey, don't start with me. This was Cecily's idea." Frieda pulled her hair back from her face and snuggled into the seat. She seemed undaunted by Helen's anger.

"What do you mean? Cecily told me last night you weren't coming to the funeral." As soon as she'd said the words, Helen hoped Frieda wouldn't ask her about the previous night.

Fortunately, Frieda was too full of her own information to notice — or perhaps she chose to ignore Helen's remark. "I'm going with you to the Bennett house."

"What?" Helen stared in disbelief. Frieda flinched as Helen shouted, "I don't know where you got the idea to join me in a little bit of breaking and entering, but you're crazy. It's not happening. So you can just get back in that car and turn right around."

But Frieda folded her arms across her chest in an all-too-familiar gesture. "I don't think you have a whole lot to say about it, since Cecily is paying you. Besides, it was her idea, not mine. She thought that three people might search the room better than one."

Helen leaned with both arms against the steering wheel and sighed. Her headache was coming back, and the rain was now pouring down in sheets. "This is not a quilting bee, Frieda," she said in a carefully tempered voice. "Nor is it a television cop show. This is serious."

Frieda, stiff and scowling, stared out the window. "I see nothing has changed. You still think of me as a child you can order around."

"Frieda, please! This is not about us —"

"The hell it isn't!"

The argument was cut short by the emergence of Cecily from the church. She darted through the rain to her car. "Fuck," Helen muttered as she started her own car. They'd have to fight about this later.

Chapter Eighteen

The noontime hour had just passed. Helen sat in her car, huge knots trying to work their way up from her stomach. She had to fight away the sense of panic as she looked at her two companions. Neither Frieda nor Cecily appeared to feel anything beyond an eagerness to get the whole expedition over with.

Helen sighed. "You're certain there's no one at home, Cecily?" she asked for the umpteenth time.

Cecily groaned, twisted around on the seat. "How many times do I have to say it? I'm positive.

Everyone is still at the church. Besides, you're with me. I live here, you know. How could they say anything if I invite you into the house? Jesus," she finished, muttering, turning back to face out the window.

"Well, you understand I'm doing more than paying a social call, right?" Helen was getting more and more irritated. Cecily seemed to have no idea of the gravity of what Helen was about to do. Going through Bennett's study while Cecily stood guard in the hallway was, as Helen fully realized, a desperate act. It was, in a way, admitting that she was at her wits' end. She didn't like having to make that admission to herself, even if the others didn't see it that way. Not only that — to have Frieda in on the whole thing was ridiculous.

And so here they were, in varying stages of discomfort and anxiety, not all of it a result of the covert operation they were about to put into motion. Sensing the tension in Frieda and Cecily, Helen wondered if they were each aware of what had truly taken place on their respective visits to Helen's house. Was Cecily's seeming knowledge of Frieda's overnight stay merely a guessing game? Or did they really tell each other everything, as Cecily claimed? If that was the case, then Frieda would know by now all about Cecily's attempted seduction of the previous evening. If it weren't so damned awkward it might even be funny, but Helen was in no laughing mood. The whole situation was silly — and it angered her.

She had to do something. Their eyes were fixed on her as they waited. Helen couldn't keep a caustic note out of her voice as she said, reaching for the door handle, "This is more like the Three Stooges than James Bond." She wrenched the door open and managed to keep herself from slamming it shut.

Frieda stuck her head out of the window as Cecily climbed out of the car. "Maybe I should stay out here and keep watch in case anyone else shows up."

Helen looked at her in surprise. Some of her fury must have communicated itself, because Frieda got out of the car and walked up to the front door.

"I can wait just inside, by these windows," Frieda said.

Cecily shrugged. "Suit yourself." She led the way up the graveled drive, Helen crunching heavily behind. Cecily worked the heavy lock on the front door, swung it open, then reached up to a panel on the wall to switch off an alarm system. "See?" she said triumphantly. "You'd never have managed to get in without me."

Helen refused to comment as they went down the familiar hallway to Bennett's study. She pushed away a stab of concern about Frieda, who'd melted into the gloom in the foyer, and was further annoyed when Cecily caught her glancing back toward the front room. "Don't worry," Cecily sighed, exasperated. "They'll be gone for hours. Everything will be fine."

Helen remained silent as she grabbed the key dangling from Cecily's hand. It worked noiselessly, and an instant later the door opened, rubbing against the freshly cleaned carpet. Helen found the wall switch, and the room glared into sudden light. The office was still as glossy and spotless as she remembered it.

In a corner below the long window that spanned

the wall opposite the door, Cecily pulled the drapery back to reveal a small two-drawer locked file cabinet. Helen joined her. Despite Cecily's reassurances, she didn't believe they had an unlimited amount of time for a search. This was the best place to start. Helen examined the lock — a simple affair that was easily jimmied open with a pocketknife. Helen squinted up at Cecily, who was watching with open fascination.

"Are you doing okay?" Helen asked, looking back down at the lock.

"What do you mean?"

"Well —" The drawer rattled in protest against her invasion. "You've just been through a very upsetting experience this morning. A funeral —"

"I'm fine. Why are you so concerned with my feelings all of a sudden? I'm just the spoiled rich brat, remember?" Cecily's voice had turned to steel.

Helen shook her head as she prodded her knife into the lock. This was tougher than it looked. "I think you'd better wait outside," she said.

Cecily's face fell. "But why? I want to watch!"

Helen lost it. "Look, this isn't Hollywood, where all the ends get neatly tied up in the last twenty minutes of the movie. What I'm doing is illegal, whether you're here or not. I'd appreciate it if you'd get the hell out of here and let me finish."

"Fine." Cecily's face hardened and she backed out of the room. Helen sighed, closing her eyes for a moment. Why the hell had this idea sounded so good a few hours ago? Was she that stupid? Helen reluctantly allowed herself an unwelcome vision of Frieda waiting in the living room, stationed by the bay window. Never, not even in her years as a cop, had she been in such emotional turmoil over a case.

It was no good. The lock was not going to cooperate with her knife. "Fuck," she sighed. As if the word were a talisman, the lock popped free. Relieved, Helen folded the knife shut and slid the top drawer open. There was still no sound from the hallway as she reached inside the drawer.

Here was a series of slim manila folders. The selection wasn't large — she easily removed a stack of them and placed them on the shining desk. A quick examination revealed that they all held similar information. Each bore the name of a young girl printed by hand. Inside was a brief dossier, including parents' names, the school attended, home address, even a few sentences describing personality traits. Most of the pages in each file were stamped with the imprint of Project Nightlight. As Helen read, she found the same sad tale told over and over — a history of abuse and neglect until the Project people had stepped in. Apparently, Bennett had taken a personal interest in these girls.

As she stood looking down at the pile of folders, Helen wondered why *these* kids as opposed to any others? Were these Project Nightlight's only cases? She shook her head, confused, but not wanting to take any more time to figure it out. The names, eight of them, were quickly jotted down and the files returned in the right order to the drawer.

After listening intently for a sound from the hallway, Helen opened the second drawer. Underneath a large secretarial checkbook were two or three bank statements, keys to a safe deposit box, and a thick envelope bulging with an assortment of bills. Helen was surprised at the lack of order. Surely Bennett had an accountant or bookkeeper who took care of these details. She leafed through the checkbook, noting the slipshod records Bennett kept of his personal finances. Outside of its messiness and complete lack of system, there was nothing out of the ordinary here.

Helen shook her head sharply, wishing she could focus clearly on what she was doing. As she replaced the checkbook, she noticed a slip of bright yellow paper that stuck out from the pale blue stack of checks. She cautiously opened the book to where the yellow paper was placed. It was a receipt dated nine days ago — the day Liz Bennett was killed.

The yellow tint was so bright that it hurt her eyes. Across the top was a simple black motif of an elephant striding, trunk uplifted, across the page. INDIAN BAZAAR was printed across the animal's side. A short blurb followed, announcing the fall shipment coming from Bombay. Clothing, jewelry, knickknacks and a wide variety of accessories could be had at low prices. Some kind of specialty shop. The fact that the goods were from India provided at least a tenuous connection to Liz, so Helen noted the address in the Noe Valley area, near the Castro district in San Francisco.

Just as she was scribbling down its location, sounds filtered in through the study door. Quickly she dropped the checkbook into the drawer, slid the drawer quietly shut, and pushed the lock into a closed position. She made it to the door in time to confront a very surprised Alice Bennett standing in the hallway.

Chapter Nineteen

Trapped, Helen faced both Lydia and Alice Bennett. Cecily tensed, glancing at all three faces. With a sick feeling, Helen saw Frieda standing sheepishly in the background, pressed against the wall as though she would like to sink permanently into the woodwork.

It was Lydia who broke the silence, tapping her cane against the thick pile carpet with a quiet, repetitive thud. "It's just as well I wasn't feeling up to staying at the church, don't you think? Convenient. Cecily, darling," she went on, her voice dangerously sweet, "why didn't you tell me you were having a little party?"

"Party?" Alice asked, turning to Lydia with a puzzled look.

Lydia closed her eyes in a moment of frustration and opened them to stare at Helen. Alice let out a nervous titter as Lydia turned and started down the corridor into a section of the house Helen had not yet seen. When no one made a move to follow her, Lydia twisted around to glare at them, leaning stiffly on the cane. Helen could imagine that beneath the well-tailored black silk suit were slender brittle bones, the skin stretched tight and pale over arthritic joints. In the dim light of the hall, the sarcastic smile leered at them.

"Isn't anyone going to join me in a drink?" she said.

In an awkward shuffle, they began to move down the hall. Helen slipped the notebook into her pocket as she took up the rear of the procession. Frieda's mouth noiselessly formed words asking what they should do next. Helen shrugged slightly and jerked her head forward, indicating that they should simply follow Lydia's lead. Cecily had a maddening, amused expression on her pert face as if she were thoroughly enjoying every moment of this confrontation.

Their brief march led them into a spacious room which opened up into light and air after the dark closeness of the hallway. The sitting room was comfortably furnished with low-lying sofas and armchairs uniformly upholstered in soft neutral colors. The deep polish of the hardwood floor reflected their movements as they all trooped in behind Lydia. An enormous skylight allowed the afternoon sunshine to illuminate even the bookshelves lining the walls. The fireplace, sheathed in cast iron, would have held a comforting glow earlier in the year. Despite the seeming warmth of the room, Helen felt a chill as they gathered there. It was as if a model home had been opened up for viewing — Helen fantasized a designer only moments ago whisking away sheets and protective coverings so that prospective buyers could be persuaded to purchase. She was sure that the room, beautiful as it was, saw little use.

"Well, come on, Alice! I'm sure we could all use a drink. All they had at that church was tea, can you believe it?" The cane waved, and Alice reluctantly moved to the bar cart tucked behind one of the longer, wider sofas. Lydia lowered herself into a wing-backed chair. "Please, sit down, all of you. We don't need to stand on ceremony." As they found places to sit, Lydia surveyed them all with a wicked gleam in her eyes. "Now then. Before I hear any ridiculous protests, I may as well tell you I know you're not a reporter like that fool who showed up the other day." Lydia took her glass from Alice as she spoke.

"You're absolutely right. I'm a private investigator."

Lydia's eyebrows raised. Alice gasped and dropped her own glass onto the carpet, spilling several fingers of very fine Scotch. Lydia glanced at Frieda who sat nervous and pale on the edge of a chair next to Helen.

Alice sopped up the mess with a tea towel. "*Two* private investigators?"

Helen ignored her. "I'm impressed. I wouldn't

131

have thought the sad death of my daughter could generate so much interest."

"No one has said what we're investigating," Helen responded, goaded by Lydia's smug manner.

"Oh, come now, young lady!" Lydia laughed. "There's no other reason for the Bennett household to arouse such excitement! Certainly not because of a faded housewife and an old bitch like myself. Don't look so hurt, Alice. It's no secret that's what we are."

Alice smiled over her refilled glass, her face a bright pink. "I don't really know what to do when she starts talking this way," she babbled to no one in particular. Helen saw Cecily blush in embarrassment. Obviously she hadn't expected an outcome like this to their harmless adventure in the world of intrigue.

"And it's no secret what these are, either," Lydia went on. She gestured toward the three younger women before her. "In my day we called them 'lezzies.' Perhaps your dear daughter can tell you, Alice, what they're called now. Dykes? Queers? So many names for a disgusting disease."

Alice's smile froze on her face as all the color drained from her cheeks. The baffled sweetness she'd been affecting faded swiftly. "For God's sake, Lydia," she breathed, the words muffled by the glass that was arrested halfway to her lips.

"Now is as good a time as any for facing the truth. If your daughter is intent on disgracing the family, it might as well be all the way." Lydia turned her eyes, green flecks of ice in a shriveled face, on Cecily. "To think that my own granddaughter would drag this — this kind of *filth* into my household! All for that poor fool Elizabeth, who didn't have the brains God gave a —"

Her tirade was cut short by a sudden spray of liquid that landed on her face and dripped down her high lace collar. Lydia gasped, her mouth gaping in soundless shock. The empty glass scuttled from Alice's grasp to the floor and rolled with a high-pitched clicking sound under the sofa. Alice followed up this gesture with an upraised hand, poised as if to slap her mother-in-law. The hand sank back down to her side. Cecily sprang up and stood between her two relatives. Both Helen and Frieda sat still.

"You old hag!" Alice screamed. Her words rocked the calm of the room with hysterical release. "Is that all you can do — throw up venom, like some — some snake? You're so full of hate and ugliness, I don't understand how you could ever bear children."

Lydia attempted to speak with quiet, icy force. "That will be enough —"

"Oh no, it won't! I haven't even started yet!" With a delirious look of excitement, almost happiness, Alice turned, took a step closer to Helen. "You want to know about Liz? I'll tell you about Liz. She hated this family and everything they stood for!" One hand pointed backwards, fingers shaking, at Lydia. "She especially hated that bitch. I heard her say it myself. Liz Bennett was the only decent human being this family ever produced, and now she's dead."

"Alice!" Lydia's hand went to her throat, fingering the fichu that now reeked of alcohol. "I'm warning you —"

"Or else what? You'll throw me out, like you did

Liz last week?" Her thin chest heaving beneath the string of pearls, Alice turned back to Lydia. "Come on, old woman, deny that one! Deny that you turned your own daughter away from this house right before she died!"

Lydia sat like a broken doll on the sofa, her thin legs splayed out, the cane resting useless by her side. Cold green eyes stared dully at Alice while liquor drizzled in slow silent drips from her chin onto the once immaculate silk suit.

Alice whipped around, her smirk triumphant. "That's right, she told Liz to go to hell. Right here in this very house. Bob was there, too, watching the whole thing."

"I don't know what you're talking about," Lydia protested faintly.

But Alice went on, ignoring her. "Then two days later the police called — and I knew. I knew that you sent her to her death. Whatever you think of me, whatever you think of my children, you'll always be guilty of that."

Lydia opened her mouth, closed and opened it again, as if gasping for air. When she spoke the words were strained. "She's hysterical — surely you can see that. She doesn't know what she's saying. I did no such thing. Not to my own daughter."

Alice began to laugh in hysterical peals. "Go ahead, lie, say whatever you want. We both know I'm telling the truth." Then Alice, as if exhausted by her verbal attack, sank into a chair nearby. "I just don't give a damn anymore."

"Mother, Grandma, please!"

Helen was startled. In the melee she'd forgotten that Cecily was watching the two women flinging words of hate at each other. Helen rose, uncertain whether she should leave them alone. But Lydia's words decided her.

"Get out of here. Both of you." She spoke in a whisper that somehow commanded respect. Helen felt a surge of relief as she and Frieda left the room and slipped out the front door, leaving the Bennett women in a well of misery in the beautiful living room.

Chapter Twenty

Helen persuaded Frieda to go home. There was a thin mist of wet fog in the air in San Francisco by the time Helen proceeded to the Indian market. As always, the Noe Valley district, one of San Francisco's most attractive, was flooded with tourists, shoppers and sightseers. The only parking space Helen could find was near Mission Dolores, so she grimly set out on the long uphill walk toward Castro. The closer she got, the heavier the crowds became. By the time Helen reached Diamond Street, she was out of patience and out of breath. The attractive buildings and welcoming shopfronts did nothing to alter her mood. At last she spotted the bright yellow doorway — a liver-and-black elephant rode in majestic bas-relief over the sign that read INDIAN BAZAAR.

The shop was almost empty. Perhaps most of the people wandering the Castro and Noe areas were in search of food rather than curios at this time of day. Helen took her time making her way through the aisles, breathing in the exotic scent of curry mingling oddly with some unfamiliar incense. Brightly colored packets of tea shared shelf space with jars of spices and seasonings, row after row of mysterious names. A glint of silver beckoned her to examine the trays of jewelry displayed under glass countertops. Two women, dressed in saris, bent over the cases of silver and gold strands laid out in gleaming array. Briefly their eyes met Helen's, but there was no further acknowledgment.

It wasn't until Helen reached racks of clothing that a clerk appeared. He was tall, blond and striking, with Nordic features and a muscular body that had benefited from a great deal of weightlifting. His bright yellow cotton tunic sported an elephant over the right breast. He put a smile on his face as Helen drew near. "Can I help you find something?" he asked amiably.

"I think I'll just look around a little," Helen answered, poking at one of the racks of women's shirts. The young man, whose name tag read BRIAN, leaned back against the cash register and watched her as she browsed. Helen picked out a bright red top and held it next to her in front of the mirror. As always, her square dark features looked back at her with a level, serious gaze. She could see Brian gauging her figure with mild interest.

"Have I seen you in here before?" he asked.

Helen shook her head, stretched a smile over her lips, and turned to face him. "Nope. First time," she said in what she hoped was the sprightly voice of an experienced consumer. Brian continued his assessment as she replaced the red blouse and ran her hand over the other garments. "Someone I know told me about this place."

"Oh, yeah? Who was that?"

Helen kept her eyes on the clothing as she answered. "Now, let me see. Oh, yes. I think it was Liz Bennett." She looked up at him. "Did you ever hear of her?"

Slowly Brian straightened up from his slouch. His body tensed, although his face stayed frozen, rigidly smiling. "Liz Bennett? Never heard the name before."

"Oh, that's funny. She talked a lot about this place." Helen paused over a blue dress and a pair of slacks in red and black stripes. "I think I'd like to try these on. Where are your fitting rooms?"

"Over there." Brian waved at a series of curtained stalls tucked beyond the counter. Helen folded the garments over her arm and wedged past Brian and his cash register in the direction of the stalls. At that moment, one of the two women in saris called him over to the jewelry counter. With a reluctant backward glance, Brian left Helen alone.

Helen knew she had no time to lose. From behind the curtain she could see that the women were absorbed in trying on different necklaces and bracelets, while Brian, barely concealing his agitation, kept looking toward the fitting rooms.

When he bent down under the counter for an elusive silver chain, Helen darted out of her chamber and into the narrow passageway that led to the back of the store.

She found the tiny office immediately — more a closet, really, than a workspace. The rotary telephone hung precariously on a cork wall dotted with notes, memos and yellow Post-its. A sheaf of invoices was impaled on an old-fashioned spike on one corner of the desk that nearly filled the room. Shelves reaching to the ceiling held an assortment of packing materials and envelopes. Helen stood hopelessly in the midst of the mess, feeling angry and foolish. Who the hell did she think she was, James Bond? Disgusted with herself, she started to back away when she noticed a photograph tucked above the telephone.

It was a more recent portrait of Liz Bennett than the one found in the backpack, but the green eyes and beautiful features were unmistakable. Liz was older and sadder here, standing alone in the midst of lush greenery, leaning on a pile of crag-edged rocks. Helen bent over to study the background. Had it been taken in India? The photograph itself looked fairly recent, in good condition. Helen could even make out the glint of the gold chain around the woman's neck.

As she reached out to take the picture from the wall a steely voice froze her in mid-motion. "Find anything interesting?" Brian asked. Helen was prevented from turning around by a sudden cold prodding of something hard and round in the small of her back. She felt herself go icy and hard. Just like the bad old days on the streets, she thought, when you never knew who might pull out a gun to kill you. With great effort she controlled the high pitch of fear that threatened to crack her voice.

"Yes, as a matter of fact, I did." Slowly she brought her hands down until they were resting, palms facing out, at her sides. "If you aren't careful, your customers are going to see something interesting, too," she added lamely, hoping to get him to put the gun away. "Look, I just want to talk to you about Liz — that's all."

"Don't worry. Everyone's gone but you and me, and I just locked the doors. No interruptions." He backed away a couple of steps. Helen got a strong whiff of sweat as he moved. He was just as scared as she was. "Just go back into the stall and get your things, and then get the hell out of here, all right?"

The nervous, questioning phrase told Helen all she needed to know. With an elaborate show of shrugging and holding her hands out in a Gallic gesture of compliance, Helen turned around.

In one swift motion, her body reacting more from instinct than with conscious thought, her arm came up and blocked his arm. Brian's hand smashed against the cork wall, bringing down the bulletin board with all its notes and memoranda. The telephone jangled out a discordant ring as it fell to the floor. Helen shoved her other elbow into his solar plexus as he tried to back out of her way.

The wind knocked out of him, Brian began to flail about with his one good hand. All his strength seemed to be sapped by the suddenness of Helen's attack. His weight and muscle worked against him once his body registered the blows. As Helen saw the hand that held the gun start to move upwards, she jerked her knee up into his groin. Brian buckled over, his mouth grimacing in silent pain, and the hand flexed open. A small piece of pipe fell with a clatter to the floor. In his fall he managed to upset the desk, which slid half over onto the floor, trailing a stream of paper in its wake.

Helen realized with horror the mistake she had made. She knew she hadn't done Brian any lasting damage, but it was a nasty shock to see how her old reflexes, honed by years in a uniform, could still take over. Brian looked up from the floor in a blank daze, panting for air. Helen kicked the pipe away, then helped him to his feet.

"That was a shitbrained thing to do, Brian. I really thought it was a gun." She maneuvered him to a stool and spotted a water cooler in the narrow corridor. He gulped down a cupful and she took a few deep breaths. The adrenaline was still surging through her body. She hadn't felt this way in a long time, but it felt good.

When Brian finally spoke his voice rasped out, punctuated by coughing. "I don't know who the fuck you are, or what you think you're doing, but you'd better get the hell out of here." He crumpled the paper cup, then gripped her arm in an iron fist that revealed he was still capable of fighting back. "I could have you arrested."

Helen looked down at his hand, then smiled at him. "But you won't. Because of Liz."

His color was returning. He let her arm fall away and leaned back, staring up at her with an odd expression. "How do you know Liz Bennett? Where is she? Is she all right?"

"Then you don't know."

"Know what? Look, just tell me where she is. Did she send you here?"

There was no kind way to do it. "Liz is dead."

His expression changed to disbelief. "No," he breathed. Then, in a shout, "No!" In huge wracking sobs, he wept.

Chapter Twenty-One

Helen stood off to one side while Brian controlled his tears and swallowed a strong cup of coffee. The afternoon sun was fading fast from the narrow city streets. Lights were winking on all over the Castro district. From where she stood Helen could see passersby glance into the Indian Bazaar with mild interest. One or two tried the door, apparently not believing the Closed sign she'd located and hung up there a few minutes ago. Careful to keep a distance, Helen glanced back at Brian. A dim bruise was forming on one cheek. He rubbed a stubby hand over his jaw and caught her eye. His gaze fell in a brooding study of his coffee cup.

"Are you going to be all right? Do you want to go to the emergency room or something?" she asked.

It must have been the wrong thing to say. He turned away in disgust. "Why don't you get the fuck out of here?" he muttered.

Helen ventured closer. She was pretty sure she hadn't done any real damage, except to his ego, and she couldn't suppress a flare of irritation at his pout. "Come on, Brian, you're the one who tried assaulting me! All I did was take care of myself." She perched on the edge of the desk. "All you have to do is talk to me. Then I'll go."

"How the hell was I supposed to know you were Ninja Bitch? I just wanted you to get out of here, all of you people." He tossed the cardboard cup on the floor under the desk.

Helen was alerted by his plural description. "What do you mean, 'all you people'? What other people?"

He tried to grimace but was stopped by the huge bruise forming on his lip. Gingerly touching it, he said, "Don't give me that shit. Bennett sent you, didn't he? Didn't want to do the dirty work himself. And I don't care what you say. I'm not telling you a fucking thing."

Helen stared, then shook her head. "You know what? You're absolutely right. I wouldn't trust me either." On impulse she handed him the telephone receiver. "I've got an idea. Call the police in Berkeley. The downtown station."

"Huh?" Brian was too puzzled to object. He took the receiver from her as she repeated her words.

"Go ahead. Get the number from information. Ask for Lieutenant Manuel Dominguez."

He looked up in amazement, shrugged and said. "What the hell?" A few minutes later he was listening to Manny, his eyes moving over her in suspicion, then surprise. After a few minutes of one-sided conversation, Brian handed over the receiver. "He wants to talk to you."

"My God, Helen, we can dress you up but we can't take you anywhere. What the hell is going on this time? Are you okay out there?"

"I'm fine, Manny. I can't talk right now. I'll tell you about it later. Thanks a lot." She hung up over his protests that no one ever told him anything.

Brian had folded his arms and was sitting on the stool, leaning his back against the wall. His face, his voice, were blank. "Then she really is dead."

Helen could only nod, remembering his tears.

Brian got up abruptly, sighed, ran his hands through his thick blond hair. "Then it doesn't matter anymore. There's nothing I can do for Liz now. It doesn't matter who you are, either." With that he bent over and scrabbled around under the desk, emerging after a moment with a large scrapbook. He held it in both hands carefully, almost reverently, and presented it to Helen. "Here," he said in the same dull voice.

Mystified, she took it from him. "What's this?"

"It belonged to Liz. She asked me if she could keep it here." Helen opened it. The scrapbook was quite worn — the binding cracked and slipping off in places, plastic sheeting peeling like old skin, the maroon vinyl crusted and scabrous. Cautiously, she turned a few pages as bits of tape and slivers of paper fell to the floor with each motion. It contained a hodgepodge of photographs, magazine and newspaper clippings, menus, theater programs, greeting cards. One, a yellowed and crumbling valentine, slid to the floor next to Brian's feet. He stooped and retrieved it, then handed it to Helen.

She closed the scrapbook and let it rest in her lap. "Tell me about Liz."

Brian averted his eyes as he spoke. "She got me this job," he began. "I met her on the plane. I was just coming back from New York, and my old man had been giving me hell about wasting all this money he'd been sending to me out here — you know? So she was talking to me, on the plane, telling me about this store where she knew the people. I guess she knew them in India. She lived there a long time." His voice took on an edge of wonderment at the thought of her adventurous life.

"You met her on the plane," Helen prompted, watching him closely as he fidgeted. "That's it? That's all there was?"

"All right, all right, so we screwed around a little bit. So what? It was only for a couple of nights," he said defensively. "No big deal. Neither one of us was serious. I was just — well, after that last night, I got worried."

"What do you mean? What happened?"

He hesitated. "Well — I don't want you to think she's crazy. She was just about the sanest woman I ever met. I mean she was educated, she traveled —"

"Just tell me what happened."

"Well, we were in bed. It was late, and we'd been making love. I was pretty tired, so I fell asleep." His voice fell, and Helen had to lean forward, straining.

146

"I remember the television was on when I fell asleep. I think Liz was still awake. She'd been acting kind of weird all night. She'd been gone all day somewhere, and when she got back to my place she was upset. Looked like she'd been crying. I tried to get her to talk to me, but she just wouldn't." He closed his eyes in sudden anguish. "If only I'd made her tell me, right then, maybe she'd still be alive now."

"Just tell me what happened," Helen pressed him, anxious to hear the whole story before he gave in to emotion.

"Like I said, I fell asleep. The news was on, or something. I guess I kind of rolled over on her in my sleep, or put my arm around her. All of a sudden she started screaming and yelling. I just about crapped out there in the bed. She scared the hell out of me." He stared out across the empty store in horror at the memory. "Screaming at the top of her lungs for me to get away from her, she wasn't going to let me hurt her anymore. And she wasn't going to let me hurt anyone else, either."

"Those were her words, exactly?" Helen asked sharply.

Brian's brow wrinkled in thought. "Yeah, pretty much. She wasn't going to let me hurt anyone else. So I woke up pretty fast, and I could see she was having a nightmare. I shook her, tried to get her to wake up. But her eyes were wide open and she was screaming right in my face —" He broke off suddenly and shook his head. "I even slapped her, can you believe it? Christ, I just wanted her to snap out of it. She started to cry after that." He ran his hands through his hair again.

147

Helen watched him. The lines around his eyes were revealed by the glare from the light bulb suspended overhead, and she could see a bald patch shining on his scalp that no amount of careful combing could hide. He looked much older than he had an hour ago. How had Liz seen him? Helen wondered. An aging surfer with some bed space to share? A temporary safe haven in the storm she was facing with her family? Or just a massage for her ego? "Did she say anything else?" Helen asked.

Brian looked up with bleary eyes. "We went back to sleep, and the next morning she was gone. I never saw her after that."

"And all she left was this?" Helen gestured to the scrapbook.

He nodded. "No note, nothing. I figured she wanted me to have it, for some reason."

For safekeeping, Helen thought. Aloud she said, "I wonder if you'd let me borrow this for a while."

He looked at her, then at the book. Shrugging, he said, "She's not going to come back for it. I guess it's okay. There's nothing in it anyway but a lot of old stuff."

As she followed Brian up to the front of the store, Helen wondered if there was, in fact, nothing the book could tell her. Like everything else so far in this case, it might turn into a dead end. Old pictures, cuttings, crumbling memories for a crumbled life.

Brian echoed her thoughts. "I was only just getting to know her." He turned the key and let in the cool night air. "There was so much about her that was — I don't know — kind of mysterious. She had a lot of secrets."

His angular face reflected the yellow streetlights. She had started to walk away when he called her back. "Just one thing," he said as he caught up with her. "I have to know. How did she die?"

Helen weighed the possibility of lying but said, "She was stabbed to death in an empty building."

She turned away quickly so she didn't have to see his pale, horrified features. Holding the scrapbook tightly to her chest she walked as fast as she could up the dark street, back to Mission Dolores and the quiet refuge of her car.

Chapter Twenty-Two

Cecily idly poked around the small clump of items Helen pulled from the backpack. Manny hadn't asked any questions when she'd asked to hold onto it for a few hours. With a shrug and a quizzical grin he had handed it over. Now Cecily pored over the contents, looking more bored than intrigued by these meagre witnesses to a life. The scrapbook hadn't done anything to improve her mood, either. Maybe it was guilt, Helen mused — guilt because, like the rest of the Bennetts, Cecily had never tried to get to know Liz.

"At least," Helen said, "we know now where she stayed when she got to San Francisco. Brian took her in for a couple of days."

"I don't know what it is you think I'm supposed to tell you from all this junk." Cecily was sullen. She picked up a patched-up pair of jeans while her free hand pushed away the cat. Boobella had crawled up onto a vacant chair at the dining room table and she now peered, bright-eyed and alert, at the small heap of personal items displayed there.

Helen tried, and failed, to repress a small movement that belied her growing irritation with the girl. "Cecily. I've told you more than once what we're doing here. I want to know if there's anything in these clothes or other things, anything at all, that seems significant. Or that points to some kind of connection that would indicate what your aunt may have wanted to do when she got back from India."

"Jesus, look at this shit! There's nothing here, nothing at all. I don't know what you dragged me over here for." In a childish snit Cecily tossed the jeans across the room. They landed with a soft plop on the dusty glass-topped coffee table. Boobella, imagining that this was all a mysterious game for her enjoyment, darted in a black furry flash out of her chair and landed, claws ready on the pile of denim. The jeans skidded off the table onto the floor. Boobella looked embarrassed and skulked into the dining room.

In spite of the aggravation between them, Helen and Cecily caught each other smiling at this absurd display of feline foolishness. The sulk came quickly back to Cecily's features as she said, "I don't know how you think I can know anything about her. I barely remember her from when I was a kid. You probably know more about her than I do now." She got up from the table and walked restlessly around the room.

Helen, her own anger mounting, watched Cecily fiddle with odds and ends scattered on shelves, on the table, on the rickety walnut dresser that held her dishes, now rarely used. To keep from shouting Helen spoke slowly, calmly, with a control she did not feel. "Then maybe it's time for me to ask you if you really want me to go on with all this."

"What do you mean?" Cecily asked. Her hands stilled for a moment as she listened for Helen's answer.

"Exactly what I said. So far you haven't shown me any sign of real remorse that your aunt died — you haven't given me anything at all to go on. Your whole attitude has been casual."

"Casual? I'd hardly call that salary you had me agree to casual."

"I haven't seen a dime of it yet," Helen retorted.

"Maybe if you earned it instead of running all over town getting into stupid brawls you might get paid. All I've seen so far is you acting like some spy in a B-movie on the late show."

Without a word Helen got up from the table and began to collect the clothes, grabbing the jeans from the living room floor, and stuffing everything in a furious shove into the backpack. She was cold with rage, and her voice cut like steel into the silent room. "Fine. Our contract is dissolved as of now. I expect you to pay my expenses only."

"What are you so mad about?" Cecily asked, following her around the room. "I'm only telling the truth! Can you honestly say that you've turned up anything at all on my dear departed aunt?" In her anger Cecily knocked over a plate, which thudded to the floor. The cat leaped up and mewed before darting off to the kitchen.

"Your 'dear departed aunt,' was she? You don't know anything about her. You don't really care one way or another that she died. God, no one in your damned family even cared where she was all her life, what she was doing, if she was all right." Helen zipped the backpack in one swift tearing motion and tossed it onto the sofa behind her. "Just tell me one thing. Tell me why you hired me. It obviously had nothing to do with Liz Bennett. Why did you drag Frieda up to my office on Monday?"

Cecily flushed and grew quiet, turning away from Helen's anger. Surprised at her reaction, Helen stared. Then truth slowly began to dawn. She couldn't believe she hadn't seen it before. "This is not about Liz Bennett, is it?" Cecily didn't move, didn't speak. Helen persisted, "This is about someone else entirely."

"I don't know what you mean."

"Oh yes, you do." Helen walked over to where Cecily stood. "Somehow this is all tied up with Frieda, isn't it?" She was right behind Cecily — she could hear her breathing, feel her warmth, the tension growing in her body.

"Dammit, I couldn't think of any other way!" Cecily burst out, turning around so suddenly that she and Helen stumbled against each other. "All she could talk about was you — your life together, all the things you did, how wonderful you were, how many good times you'd had! Not in so many words all the time. But I could see it, all the memories, all the life you'd shared, all the love you had. You had each other. I didn't have anything. Nothing Frieda wanted, anyway."

Helen had backed off a few paces from Cecily. Now she said in a gentle voice, "I don't understand. What did coming to my office have to do with any of that?"

"You don't get it? I had to meet you. I had to get to know you. When my aunt was killed, Frieda got all jazzed up about you, how you'd be able to figure it out. What a good detective you were. Then she said —" Cecily broke off, her face red.

"What did she say?"

"After all that she got really quiet. Then she said how sorry she was for giving you such a hard time about being a private eye." Cecily's voice fell and Helen strained to hear her. "I really hated you that night, you know? I didn't even know you, and I hated you so much."

"And you loved Frieda." Helen felt an odd detachment as she said the words, as if this scene were taking place far away from them both. The encroaching darkness outside, painting the windows black, only heightened the sense of unreality.

"I thought I did. I had to meet you, somehow — to see what she was so crazy about." Cecily moved closer, and Helen was uncomfortably aware of her body, her breathing. Her hand reached out, tentative, trembling, to find Helen's. "I saw it right away."

"Cecily, Cecily — this is insane." Even as she said the words, Helen felt her own body respond. It had a will of its own as it let Cecily's hand stroke her arm, then find her shoulder and neck. "You don't know what you're talking about. You're just upset. I'm upset. That's all this is." But Helen could not deny the way her own breathing quickened. Each caress of Cecily's seemed to leave a glowing trace on her skin. When their lips touched the gesture was gentle, almost frightened. Slowly their mouths opened, and Helen pulled Cecily to her in a violent motion.

"We shouldn't," Helen murmured into Cecily's neck.

"I know."

They kissed again. Helen could feel Cecily's breasts pressing against her own. Suddenly their hands were pulling at clothes with urgency, forcing their way to the feel of warm skin. Helen opened her eyes to find Cecily leading her to the sofa.

"I don't give a damn." She pulled Helen down on top of her with rough abandon, her smile triumphant.

Helen saw the gleam of conquest in her wide green eyes. For a moment Helen hesitated. But then she deliberately pushed the uncertainty away. To conceal her doubt she kissed Cecily hard, her mouth pushing, insistent. Cecily moaned, first in surprise, then in excitement.

"I've dreamed about this every night since the first time I saw you." Cecily sighed.

Helen reached for the lamp and the living room disappeared in darkness. She didn't trust herself to respond. She knew that in a little while she wouldn't believe anything Cecily had said. But for now she didn't care if it was all lies. She was tired of fighting off memories, tired of doing her best, tired of pretending to be fine. No more. Not tonight.

"Shut up," she said flatly to Cecily. "Don't try to make this any more than what it is."

"And just what do you think it is?" Cecily's voice was warm and teasing.

For some reason Helen didn't care to examine, the question made her angry. As an answer she buried her face on Cecily's breasts.

Chapter Twenty-Three

When the telephone rang Helen grabbed it quickly, clumsily, as if afraid that Cecily would try to answer. Cecily, however, barely looked up from her perusal of the morning paper. She briefly scowled at Helen over her orange juice. Glad of the interruption to their breakfast, Helen was relieved to hear Manny's voice.

"So — did you get finished with the stuff?" he asked in his best bright sunshiny morning voice. It was the same voice Helen used to hate when they worked together.

"Yeah, yeah. I'll bring it over in a little while."

"Ah, still getting up on the wrong side of the bed, I see."

Helen was silent, embarrassed to remember that she hadn't gotten up out of a bed at all this morning. Instead, there had been a cramped, uneasy night exhausted on the sofa, with Cecily curled up in her arms.

"Hello?"

"Oh. Sorry." Helen turned so Cecily couldn't see her face. "Don't worry. I'll bring it around this morning."

"Everything all right?"

"Of course. Why, do I sound as if it's not?"

"Yes, a bit. Wait a minute. I get it. You're not alone, are you?"

"Listen, I'll see you in a few minutes, okay?" She was about to hang up when he sputtered out a protest.

"Hang on a second, that's why I'm calling. I'm not at home right now."

"Oh?" A confused explanation followed, outlining why he'd had to come in to the station early to finish up a report that hadn't been filled out properly. Helen paid scant attention to him, wondering instead how to get Cecily out of the house and worrying about the consequences of the previous night.

"Did you hear a single thing I said?" Manny was asking. "What's going on over there?"

Helen snapped back, "Yes, I heard. You want me to drop the bag off tonight instead of this morning."

"Jesus. Next time call up some other old pal to do you favors."

Helen relented. "I'm sorry, Manny. I'll explain when I see you," she finished limply. Cecily was still staring at the paper with great concentration. Apparently she hadn't paid attention to the phone call. Helen breathed a small sigh of relief as she hung up, but she felt nervous when Cecily turned sleepy eyes in her direction.

"I can't believe this crap," Cecily sneered. "You should read this article. It's all about Daddy."

"Malone?" Helen asked.

"No, this is the San Francisco paper. Listen, they're talking about Aunt Liz here, wondering where Daddy was the night she died. They know damned well he was giving that speech on Tuesday night. All of us were there."

Helen cast her mind back to the information Manny had given her several days ago. "Tuesday night. The speech was at the university, right?"

"You'd think they'd be tired of the Bennett family by now. At least it's not on the front page anymore."

Helen shrugged. "You know the press. Don't worry about it." At the moment she was more concerned with how to get Cecily to leave. It had been a long time since she'd had to deal with someone sleeping over. She'd forgotten how uncomfortable the following morning could be. This time there was also the added problem of Frieda. If Cecily did indeed tell Frieda everything, then last night's adventure would be shared knowledge in a matter of hours. Right now Helen felt too angry with herself and confused at the whole mess to feel equal to a charming and leisurely breakfast with the woman she'd made love to last night.

Brooding, she realized that Cecily was still

griping about the newspaper article. "And they even mention the way the schedule of speakers got messed up that night! As if that was his fault or something. God." She picked up the paper again. "This is ridiculous. I'm going to write a letter to the editor, or call them, or something." She got up from the table and started prowling around the kitchen. "Don't you have a pencil or paper around anywhere?"

"Here." Helen picked up a small pad with a pen clipped to the cover. "Go ahead, although I don't think it's the article that's bothering you."

"What do you mean?" Cecily was already flipping through pages of newsprint.

"I get the feeling you're just as uneasy as I am about last night." Helen pushed aside her coffee and leaned over on the table. "Aren't you?"

Cecily managed a smile. "Maybe." Doodling on the notebook, she added, "I don't usually get so worked up about things like this."

"No? I guess that's kind of a compliment."

Cecily hung her head. "I feel awful. No, no," she protested, glancing up at Helen. "You weren't awful. Just the opposite. I was awful. To both you and Frieda."

"Hey, I'm over twenty-one. It was as much my choice as yours." Helen gazed at the green eyes and beautiful pale skin with mixed feelings of longing and sorrow. "But I think I'd better make a choice right now not to let it happen again."

"Because of Frieda?" Helen was surprised to see hurt appear in Cecily's eyes.

"Not entirely. I think the biggest reason is that we're too much alike. We both enjoy being in control too much. You want to control both me and Frieda

— and I — well, I have enough trouble just controlling my own life."

Helen watched her as she let the pen trace idly across a sheet of paper. They were both silent for a few moments.

Helen forced a laugh. "Don't look so tragic about it. I'm not sorry for making love to you. I'm just sorry that it has to stop where it is."

"I'm not sorry either," Cecily said. She was smiling but still avoiding Helen's eyes. The pen occupied her hands and her attention. Helen was suddenly reminded of her dream — the woman, sitting alone in Bennett's study, writing in the strange white light. Cecily even resembled the woman, and the dream image that was Liz Bennett. Helen's gaze moved to Cecily's hands, and the same frustration she'd felt in the dream stole over her again. The pen moved slowly, creating meaningless scratches on the page, and Helen stared as if hypnotized by the motion.

"Helen? Are you okay? You're scaring me." Helen started at the note of fear in Cecily's voice.

"I was just thinking," Helen answered, and her voice trailed off.

"About what? You look like you blanked out or something."

"Maybe I did." Helen got up abruptly and walked into the living room. The backpack was still sitting where she'd left it, flung onto the floor last night. She sat down and without ceremony began tossing Liz Bennett's personal belongings aside, scattering them all around her.

With a puzzled frown, Cecily followed and watched. "Have you completely lost your mind?"

"Here it is." Helen held it up for Cecily to see. Cecily knelt down beside her and took the gold pencil from Helen's outstretched hand. "It was in the backpack found where your aunt's body was discovered."

"A pencil? You have lost it."

"No, no. Look at it. Does that look like something your aunt would have carried around?" Helen picked up the clothing, the well-worn hairbrush.

"Well, no, not exactly, but I don't understand —"

"I do. Finally, I do understand." Helen stuffed everything but the pencil back into the bag. "Something is finally starting to make sense."

"But wait!" Cecily scrambled to her feet and started after Helen. "Aren't you going to tell me what the hell you're talking about?"

Helen paused. "I don't know if you'll want to hear what I think, Cecily. Besides, I can't prove anything. No, not yet — I can't tell you yet."

"For God's sake, Helen! At least tell me where you're going!" Cecily followed her to the front door, where Helen was already slipping into a jacket and grabbing her shoulder bag.

"Where are my keys? Oh, here." She pulled them, rattling, from her pocket. She turned back, hand on the open door, to Cecily. "I'm sorry. I know I must seem crazy."

"You're still on my payroll, you know. You're supposed to tell me what you find out." Cecily tried to sound tough but succeeded only in appearing frightened. Helen took her hand and held it tight. "I may have to fire you."

Helen let her hand go. "You'll probably want to do more than that, if I'm right."

"Can't I come along?" Cecily asked. "I promise to behave."

"Not this time. I'll be back. You can stay here as long as you want." Helen left Cecily standing in the doorway.

Chapter Twenty-Four

Robert Bennett sat enthroned, as before, behind the huge desk. He regarded Helen with a mixture of interest and politely concealed disgust. "I can't imagine what else you have to say to me. Not after that little display the other day with the reporter — what's his name — Malone? That washed-up old ass! And now my mother tells me that you aren't even a reporter." He leaned back grandly in the chair, pressed his fingertips together, and smiled at her. "Maybe you wouldn't mind telling me what this is all about."

Instead of responding, Helen looked around the room. "Where is your mother, by the way?"

His eyebrows went up in surprise. "Not that it's any of your business, but she happens to be resting. She's not a well woman, as I'm sure even you could tell. Why do you want to know?"

Helen stood near the desk, the surface of which was nearly bare, except for a virginally white blotter, a pen, and a small sheaf of notes. Behind Bennett's chair hung a new photograph, a blowup of the one taken the night of the reception at the Clarion. The little girl faced the camera as she rested in Bennett's arms. His fingers splayed over her exposed thigh, and he was smiling at her, a wise, knowing, adult smile.

Helen looked from the photograph into Bennett's green eyes, so startlingly similar to those of his daughter. "Why did you agree to see me, anyway?"

He shrugged, began to look irritated. "Curiosity, really. However, this is all getting tiresome. If all you want to do is gawk around the room, perhaps you'll be good enough to —"

Helen cut him off as he rose from his chair. "Interesting picture," she said, nodding at the wall. "Revealing, wouldn't you say?"

Despite his assured manner and gracious voice there was a small twitch at his temple. "I don't know what you mean."

"Well, I bet the little girls in your secret file would be able to tell me, wouldn't they? Or maybe Liz. *If* she were alive to talk about it."

He paled, frozen behind the desk. "I think you ought to leave now," he said in a tight voice.

Helen scuffed at the carpet with her shoe,

leaving deep welts in the fabric. "When did you clean this carpet, Bennett? Was it the same night Liz died here? Or the next day, maybe? You had to cover up the blood somehow."

He struggled to speak. Fear and rage battled across his face, but the only sound he made was a ragged gasp. Helen felt her revulsion rising at the man collapsed in the chair behind the desk. She walked quickly across the room and loomed over him. "It happened right here, in this room," she said in a low voice. "What did she do that ticked you off? Did she threaten to tell what you had in mind for those special little Project Nightlight girls? Did she say she'd tell the world what you did to her while she was growing up?"

"You can't — you can't prove anything." Cringing, he slid down in the chair. "No one would ever believe you."

Helen backed off. "Maybe not. Maybe they wouldn't believe her, either." She looked around the room, talking more to herself than to him. "Is that what drew her back here that night? Looking for some kind of proof, some way to stop you."

"No one in my family has seen Liz for years! Not since she ran off on one of her idiotic schemes!"

"Really? Then who was it your wife saw in this study last week?"

As she walked around the room, going farther away from him, Bennett seemed to gain a little courage. "You're crazy!" he cried out. "Don't think for a minute you can stop me, or my work. What I do is good, and important. I don't hurt people. I help them!"

"Sure — the same way you helped Liz, when you

were kids. Did you know she had nightmares about you? Terrified of you touching her?"

It seemed to be working. Ever since that first visit, it was clear to Helen that Bennett without his mother had no strength or will to fight. If she could just have a few minutes more with him, she would be able to persuade him to call the police, or —

"That will do, Robert." Lydia's steely voice, though quiet, seemed to ring with bell-like clarity through the room. Helen turned from Bennett, angry at herself. Of all the stupid things to do, she thought, this was the worst. Her own arrogance had led her into this ambush. Slowly she faced the head of the Bennett family.

Lydia was, as always, dressed impeccably in a suit of neutral color. Today she wore a pearl choker above the white silk blouse, hiding her withered throat beneath a row of gems. The gray steel of the gun protruding from her hand seemed almost comical, but the grip was calm, unshaking. Helen's gaze moved up from the gun to the sharp, familiar features of the Bennett face.

Lydia shut the door behind her as quietly as she'd opened it. "It was that damned pencil, wasn't it? I couldn't find it that night, no matter where we looked." She swiveled stiffly to glare at her son. "I told you we'd have to find it. Cleaning the carpets and the desk wasn't enough." The gun jerked up. Helen froze. "Out with it! Tell me!"

Helen managed to find words to force through her dry mouth. "The pencil got into the backpack. It was there with her other things. I noticed the pen the day I was here with Malone. And the room itself — it was just too clean . . ." Helen's words trailed off as she frantically searched her brain for a way to get that gun away without anyone getting hurt.

Lydia heaved a deep sigh, the lace at her neck quivering. "You can't prove any of this. You have no evidence." She stated it calmly, sorting it out for herself. "Even the pencil doesn't prove anything. I can only assume that you hoped to weaken and frighten this son of mine into making some kind of confession."

Bennett suddenly burst out, "But it wasn't me, Mother! Tell her, it wasn't me!" He stood, hands fluttering before him in a pleading gesture. "I just helped you clean it up. I didn't do it."

"Shut up, fool! For God's sake, keep your damned mouth shut!" The pistol came up from Lydia's side, then lowered again. The cold green eyes pierced her own, hate and contempt emanating from her in waves. "It doesn't matter. Anything you heard here is never going to be believed. Face it — your plan didn't work, Helen Black, private investigator." A smile crept across her lips. "You've failed."

The smile faded as Helen, her voice coming back, began to speak. "It was you, then. It was you, wasn't it, Lydia? You must have surprised her in here, that night, while she was looking for evidence. Some way to keep Bennett from going on with his beloved little project."

"That's nonsense! My son was speaking that night at the university!"

"But the schedule was changed. Cecily told me it was. He didn't speak at the time when he was supposed to, did he?"

Behind her Bennett moaned. "Mother, she

knows," he whimpered. "She knows about the speech, she knows we came back for my notes __"

"She doesn't know a damned thing!"

Helen faced Bennett, hoping to take advantage of his shaken state. "How did Lydia get the knife? She was too weak to put up a fight with Liz. Was it just sitting on the desk, or did Lydia find it in the backpack?"

"It — it just fell out of the bag thing she had, right on the floor. I never touched it," Bennett stammered. "Tell her, Mother, it was you. You all the time." He went to her side, pleading. "Please, Mother!"

All the while Helen had been moving closer, trying to get into a better position, keeping one eye on Lydia's gun. As Lydia listened, her attention wavered, and the mouth of the pistol fell slightly, away from its focus on Helen. With Bennett's coming out from behind the desk, gesturing and pleading, Helen stood behind him. Now Lydia's son faced the gun.

Lydia's face crumpled as her offspring cowered. "All my life," she said, "all my life I've done everything I could for you. If it weren't for me you wouldn't even get to *look* at the governor, much less be his best friend. And this is how you thank me? By displaying your shame for all the world to see?"

"My shame?" Astonishment, then rage, distorted his features. "My shame? You're the one who killed your own daughter!"

"And you're the one who raped her! Don't get high and mighty with me, Robert Bennett! This family would be nowhere if you'd been running it!"

"So that's what we are to you — a machine to be run. We're not your own flesh and blood?"

The quiet whisper of the door opening stopped all of them. Helen had no idea how much Cecily had heard. Apparently, though, it was more than enough, given her white, shocked face and tear-filled eyes.

"Cecily — Cecily, darling," Lydia began, her voice trembling and faint.

Without a word Cecily walked into the room and took the gun from her grandmother. She handed it to Helen. "Here. Do whatever you want with it."

Chapter Twenty-Five

"But how did Cecily know where you had gone?" Frieda asked.

Helen took up the half-empty bottle of wine. There was enough to refill each of their glasses. She took her time pouring, weighing the words of her answer carefully. "Cecily had been going over the stuff in the backpack and scrapbook with me," Helen said, "and it was only then that the gold pencil struck me. I knew I'd seen something like it before. What I'd seen was the matching pen, in Bob Bennett's study."

Frieda seemed satisfied and raised no questions about Cecily's presence in Helen's house. "So she followed you back to her house?"

"Right," Helen said, inwardly relaxing, relieved. Maybe in spite of her honesty policy, Cecily hadn't told Frieda anything about their night together. "I didn't want her there with me when I confronted her father. I thought it would just confuse things, make him more reluctant to talk to me."

Frieda took another sip of wine and shook her head as she savored it. "I'm surprised he saw you at all. Especially since he knew you were investigating Liz Bennett's death."

"Me, too. I think he was hoping to learn more about what I'd found out. Especially after Lydia told him I'd been going through his study."

"I still can't believe that Cecily's grandmother could have killed her own daughter! She's such an old, frail-looking woman. Besides, how can you do that to your own child?"

Helen laughed bitterly. "Parents hurt their kids all the time, Frieda. And in spite of how it must look, I think it really was an accident. Lydia probably just grabbed the knife when it fell out of the backpack, meaning to threaten her daughter with it. Good old Bob Bennett must have shit bricks when Lydia told him they'd have to figure out something to do with the body." Helen shuddered as she recalled Lydia's words while they had waited for the police to arrive — cramming the body in the trunk of Lydia's car, driving the car back to the campus where Bob gave a short and incoherent speech, then finally, hours later, dumping their

172

gruesome cargo in the Darcy Building. "Bob dragged Liz into the place, then replaced the knife in her back to make it look like a random killing," Helen went on. "I guess they figured no one would come across the body in there for weeks, maybe months."

Frieda sighed. "Unbelievable. But what made you realize what was wrong with Bennett in the first place?"

"Two things, really. Those files on the girls. It was as if he'd handpicked a harem for himself. Being in charge of Project Nightlight — God, what a name! — was like giving him a license to play his little pedophilic games. And then there was Liz's nightmare, too. When I saw that photograph, the way he was holding the little girl, it all clicked into place." She stopped when she felt Frieda's eyes searching her face. The memory of what had taken place only hours ago on the same sofa where they now sat checked Helen's desire to touch her, to stroke her hair and embrace her. Helen blushed at the rough groping Cecily had inspired.

"You okay?" Frieda asked as she moved nearer, her voice warm and sympathetic.

"Yeah." Helen tried to laugh it off. "It's just been a difficult week for me."

"Well, what happens to the Bennetts now?"

Helen was about to answer when the doorbell rang. She groaned, rolled her eyes. "I'd better see who it is," she murmured The cat, alert and excited, followed her. Cecily stood there, a wry smile on her face, an envelope in her hand. She offered it to Helen.

Helen glanced at the dollar amount on the check

before replacing it in the envelope. "We could have taken care of this later, Cecily. You've got a lot more important things to do right now than pay bills."

Cecily snorted. She had aged in the last twenty-four hours. The bright green eyes flashed hard at Helen, and her skin stretched taut and brittle over the bones. "I think you've earned it," she said, pushing Helen's hand away. "Frieda's with you, isn't she?"

"Yes. Would you — would you like to come —"

Cecily held both hands up in mock horror. "God, no. Let's leave you two lovebirds alone, shall we? Don't worry, I didn't tell her about our wild night of lust on the couch."

The moments passed in painful silence. Desperate for something to say, Helen blurted out, "How is your family doing?" Instantly she knew it was the wrong thing to say, but it was too late to take the words back.

"Family? What family? Jane moved in with her junkie boyfriend. Mother is in a padded cell in Napa. Grandma is in the hospital and not expected to last much more than a couple of weeks. Daddy is out on bail and locked up with a bunch of lawyers from the governor's office. Anything else you want to know?"

Helen hung her head as she listened to this brief diatribe, wishing she could ease the hurt that distorted Cecily's face. "I'm so sorry. I never meant to hurt you."

Cecily ignored her. "I see," she said, "by the papers that you've given Malone an exclusive interview. The two of you managed to carve us all up pretty well."

"I thought I owed it to him." Helen took a step

174

closer to her. Cecily jerked back, avoiding her touch. "He helped me quite a lot."

"Payback time, huh? Well, I hope you both enjoy yourselves."

"Come on, Cecily. This has not exactly been a vacation. It's my job. This is what I do for a living." Helen immediately regretted the anger that had seeped into her voice, but it was too late. Cecily was already marching from the tiny porch in the direction of her car.

"Fine. Then you can take your money and leave me alone."

"This is more than we agreed to." Helen realized she must look like some character in a play, a melodrama, standing on the porch with outstretched hand, waving the envelope at the retreating figure in the driveway.

"Then donate it to charity. Open up a trust account for your cat. Or shove it up your ass. I don't give a flying fuck what you do with it." In a screech of tires and a whirl of dust and exhaust she was gone.

Helen didn't have to turn around to know that Frieda was standing behind her. "That was Cecily, wasn't it?"

"Right." Helen folded the envelope into a thick hard square and stuffed it into her pocket. Frieda's expression showed only concern. How much had she heard? "She's upset right now."

"Understatement of the year, I'd say. What are you going to do with it? The money, I mean."

"I don't know yet. Cecily would probably call it blood money. Hell, maybe all the money I get is blood money — raking a living off of other people's problems." She saw Frieda shiver. Night was suddenly upon them, and light and warmth had faded from the day. Still Helen lingered on the porch, uneasy. "Did Cecily ever talk to you about me?"

Frieda smiled and stroked Helen's arm. "I know she flirted with you a little. Don't worry. I didn't really tell her anything about the other night."

Helen stared, but Frieda's face was entirely innocent. It was the same emotional battleground. How much honesty could they stand? Just one more lie, one more little hypocrisy to add to their history. Was it worth it?

"It's getting cold. Let's go inside." Frieda picked up the cat and led Helen back into the house. The door closed, firm and solid, against the darkness.

Chapter Twenty-Six

Helen stood in the cemetery at St. Monica's under a late September sun. Four months had passed since she'd last been here. Berkeley was unusually hot. You never knew how the weather would be at this time of year — either fog-covered, or baking in the last throes of summer. She fought the urge to take off her dark blue jacket and tried instead to listen to the young priest as he finished the burial rite.

Only Cecily and Helen were there to watch Lydia Bennett's coffin be lowered into the ground. As she tossed her spade of soil into the grave, Helen saw that the earth covering Liz Bennett had just begun to settle. A few rows of pale green grass were growing there. The priest shook hands with Cecily and murmured a few words to her. Cecily nodded, gave a brief smile, then slowly walked away. Helen followed, noting how thin she'd grown under her lightweight black dress. She looked frail as she walked among the gravestones.

Once the priest had gone back into the church, Cecily stopped and waited for Helen. "Why are you here?" she asked in a quiet voice.

Helen shook her head. "I'm not sure, Cecily. Maybe I just felt it was one last piece of business I had with the Bennett family."

They continued in silence to the sidewalk. Cecily's shoes clacked on the hot paving stones. "Daddy's trial starts next week," she said.

"I know. I'll be testifying. I'm sure you will, too."

When they reached the parking lot Cecily waited while Helen took off her jacket and tossed it onto the back seat of her car. "As soon as the trial is over," Cecily said, "I'm getting out of here."

"Probably the best thing. Where will you go?"

"Not that it's any of your business, but I'm going back to UC Santa Cruz in January. Might as well finish my degree." Cecily leaned against Helen's car and sighed. "I guess I have to hang around for the holidays. Mother will be out of the looney bin for a while at Christmas, and Jane might show up."

"Cecily, if there's anything I can do —"

"No one expected Grandma to hang on as long as she did," Cecily interrupted. "The old bitch was tough."

"For what it's worth, you know how to get in touch with me," Helen said. "Or Frieda. We'd be glad to help you any way we can."

" 'We'? You both have the same address these days, I take it."

"That's right."

Cecily moved away from Helen. "Frieda and I never would have lasted. Probably just as well." Her eyes roamed over the cemetery laid out before them. "You know, Project Nightlight bit the dust right after they arrested Daddy. It'll probably never see the light of day."

"I'm sorry to hear that. It was a good idea."

"Yeah, well, we took care of that, didn't we? I'm glad Grandma is dead and buried. Maybe that's where all the Bennetts should be, for all the misery we've created." She turned on her heel and fled to her car.

Helen waited until Cecily was out of sight before she headed for home.

A few of the publications of
THE NAIAD PRESS, INC.
P.O. Box 10543 • Tallahassee, Florida 32302
Phone (904) 539-5965
Mail orders welcome. Please include 15% postage.

CURIOUS WINE by Katherine V. Forrest. 176 pp. Tenth
Anniversary Edition. The most popular contemporary Lesbian
love story.   ISBN 1-56280-053-1 $9.95

CHAUTAUQUA by Catherine Ennis. 192 pp. Exciting, romantic
adventure.   ISBN 1-56280-032-9   9.95

A PROPER BURIAL by Pat Welch. 192 pp. Third in the Helen
Black mystery series.   ISBN 1-56280-033-7   9.95

SILVERLAKE HEAT: A Novel of Suspense by Carol Schmidt.
240 pp. Rhonda is as hot as Laney's dreams.   ISBN 1-56280-031-0   9.95

LOVE, ZENA BETH by Diane Salvatore. 224 pp. The most talked
about lesbian novel of the nineties!   ISBN 1-56280-030-2   9.95

A DOORYARD FULL OF FLOWERS by Isabel Miller. 160 pp.
Stories incl. 2 sequels to Patience and Sarah. ISBN 1-56280-029-9   9.95

MURDER BY TRADITION by Katherine V. Forrest. 288 pp. A
Kate Delafield Mystery. 4th in a series.   ISBN 1-56280-002-7   9.95

THE EROTIC NAIAD edited by Katherine V. Forrest & Barbara Grier.
224 pp. Love stories by Naiad Press authors.   ISBN 1-56280-026-4   12.95

DEAD CERTAIN by Claire McNab. 224 pp. 5th Det. Insp. Carol
Ashton mystery.   ISBN 1-56280-027-2   9.95

CRAZY FOR LOVING by Jaye Maiman. 320 pp. 2nd Robin
Miller mystery.   ISBN 1-56280-025-6   9.95

STONEHURST by Barbara Johnson. 176 pp. Passionate regency
romance.   ISBN 1-56280-024-8   9.95

INTRODUCING AMANDA VALENTINE by Rose Beecham.
256 pp. An Amanda Valentine Mystery — 1st in a series.
                                              ISBN 1-56280-021-3   9.95

UNCERTAIN COMPANIONS by Robbi Sommers. 204 pp.
Steamy, erotic novel.   ISBN 1-56280-017-5   9.95

A TIGER'S HEART by Lauren W. Douglas. 240 pp. Fourth Caitlin
Reece Mystery.   ISBN 1-56280-018-3   9.95

PAPERBACK ROMANCE by Karin Kallmaker. 256 pp. A
delicious romance.   ISBN 1-56280-019-1   9.95

MORTON RIVER VALLEY by Lee Lynch. 304 pp. Lee Lynch at her best! ISBN 1-56280-016-7 9.95

THE LAVENDER HOUSE MURDER by Nikki Baker. 224 pp. A Virginia Kelly Mystery. Second in a series. ISBN 1-56280-012-4 9.95

PASSION BAY by Jennifer Fulton. 224 pp. Passionate romance, virgin beaches, tropical skies. ISBN 1-56280-028-0 9.95

STICKS AND STONES by Jackie Calhoun. 208 pp. Contemporary lesbian lives and loves. ISBN 1-56280-020-5 9.95

DELIA IRONFOOT by Jeane Harris. 192 pp. Adventure for Delia and Beth in the Utah mountains. ISBN 1-56280-014-0 9.95

UNDER THE SOUTHERN CROSS by Claire McNab. 192 pp. Romantic nights Down Under. ISBN 1-56280-011-6 9.95

RIVERFINGER WOMEN by Elana Nachman/Dykewomon. 208 pp. Classic Lesbian/feminist novel. ISBN 1-56280-013-2 8.95

A CERTAIN DISCONTENT by Cleve Boutell. 240 pp. A unique coterie of women. ISBN 1-56280-009-4 9.95

GRASSY FLATS by Penny Hayes. 256 pp. Lesbian romance in the '30s. ISBN 1-56280-010-8 9.95

A SINGULAR SPY by Amanda K. Williams. 192 pp. 3rd spy novel featuring Lesbian agent Madison McGuire. ISBN 1-56280-008-6 8.95

THE END OF APRIL by Penny Sumner. 240 pp. A Victoria Cross Mystery. First in a series. ISBN 1-56280-007-8 8.95

A FLIGHT OF ANGELS by Sarah Aldridge. 240 pp. Romance set at the National Gallery of Art ISBN 1-56280-001-9 9.95

HOUSTON TOWN by Deborah Powell. 208 pp. A Hollis Carpenter mystery. Second in a series. ISBN 1-56280-006-X 8.95

KISS AND TELL by Robbi Sommers. 192 pp. Scorching stories by the author of *Pleasures*. ISBN 1-56280-005-1 9.95

STILL WATERS by Pat Welch. 208 pp. Second in the Helen Black mystery series. ISBN 0-941483-97-5 9.95

MURDER IS GERMANE by Karen Saum. 224 pp. The 2nd Brigid Donovan mystery. ISBN 0-941483-98-3 8.95

TO LOVE AGAIN by Evelyn Kennedy. 208 pp. Wildly romantic love story. ISBN 0-941483-85-1 9.95

IN THE GAME by Nikki Baker. 192 pp. A Virginia Kelly mystery. First in a series. ISBN 01-56280-004-3 9.95

AVALON by Mary Jane Jones. 256 pp. A Lesbian Arthurian romance. ISBN 0-941483-96-7 9.95

STRANDED by Camarin Grae. 320 pp. Entertaining, riveting adventure. ISBN 0-941483-99-1 9.95

THE DAUGHTERS OF ARTEMIS by Lauren Wright Douglas. 240 pp. Third Caitlin Reece mystery. ISBN 0-941483-95-9 9.95

CLEARWATER by Catherine Ennis. 176 pp. Romantic secrets
of a small Louisiana town.   ISBN 0-941483-65-7   8.95

THE HALLELUJAH MURDERS by Dorothy Tell. 176 pp.
Second Poppy Dillworth mystery.   ISBN 0-941483-88-6   8.95

ZETA BASE by Judith Alguire. 208 pp. Lesbian triangle
on a future Earth.   ISBN 0-941483-94-0   9.95

SECOND CHANCE by Jackie Calhoun. 256 pp. Contemporary
Lesbian lives and loves.   ISBN 0-941483-93-2   9.95

BENEDICTION by Diane Salvatore. 272 pp. Striking,
contemporary romantic novel.   ISBN 0-941483-90-8   9.95

CALLING RAIN by Karen Marie Christa Minns. 240 pp.
Spellbinding, erotic love story   ISBN 0-941483-87-8   9.95

BLACK IRIS by Jeane Harris. 192 pp. Caroline's hidden past . . .
                                          ISBN 0-941483-68-1   8.95

TOUCHWOOD by Karin Kallmaker. 240 pp. Loving, May/
December romance.   ISBN 0-941483-76-2   9.95

BAYOU CITY SECRETS by Deborah Powell. 224 pp. A Hollis
Carpenter mystery. First in a series.   ISBN 0-941483-91-6   9.95

COP OUT by Claire McNab. 208 pp. 4th Det. Insp. Carol Ashton
mystery.   ISBN 0-941483-84-3   9.95

LODESTAR by Phyllis Horn. 224 pp. Romantic, fast-moving
adventure.   ISBN 0-941483-83-5   8.95

THE BEVERLY MALIBU by Katherine V. Forrest. 288 pp. A
Kate Delafield Mystery. 3rd in a series. ISBN 0-941483-48-7   9.95

THAT OLD STUDEBAKER by Lee Lynch. 272 pp. Andy's affair
with Regina and her attachment to her beloved car.
                                          ISBN 0-941483-82-7   9.95

PASSION'S LEGACY by Lori Paige. 224 pp. Sarah is swept into
the arms of Augusta Pym in this delightful historical romance.
                                          ISBN 0-941483-81-9   8.95

THE PROVIDENCE FILE by Amanda Kyle Williams. 256 pp.
Second espionage thriller featuring lesbian agent Madison McGuire
                                          ISBN 0-941483-92-4   8.95

I LEFT MY HEART by Jaye Maiman. 320 pp. A Robin Miller
Mystery. First in a series.   ISBN 0-941483-72-X   9.95

THE PRICE OF SALT by Patricia Highsmith (writing as Claire
Morgan). 288 pp. Classic lesbian novel, first issued in 1952 . . .
acknowledged by its author under her own, very famous, name.
                                          ISBN 1-56280-003-5   9.95

SIDE BY SIDE by Isabel Miller. 256 pp. From beloved author of
Patience and Sarah.   ISBN 0-941483-77-0   9.95

SOUTHBOUND by Sheila Ortiz Taylor. 240 pp. Hilarious sequel
to *Faultline.*   ISBN 0-941483-78-9   8.95

STAYING POWER: LONG TERM LESBIAN COUPLES
by Susan E. Johnson. 352 pp. Joys of coupledom.
ISBN 0-941-483-75-4   12.95

SLICK by Camarin Grae. 304 pp. Exotic, erotic adventure.
ISBN 0-941483-74-6   9.95

NINTH LIFE by Lauren Wright Douglas. 256 pp. A Caitlin
Reece mystery. 2nd in a series.   ISBN 0-941483-50-9   8.95

PLAYERS by Robbi Sommers. 192 pp. Sizzling, erotic novel.
ISBN 0-941483-73-8   9.95

MURDER AT RED ROOK RANCH by Dorothy Tell. 224 pp.
First Poppy Dillworth adventure.   ISBN 0-941483-80-0   8.95

LESBIAN SURVIVAL MANUAL by Rhonda Dicksion.
112 pp. Cartoons!   ISBN 0-941483-71-1   8.95

A ROOM FULL OF WOMEN by Elisabeth Nonas. 256 pp.
Contemporary Lesbian lives.   ISBN 0-941483-69-X   9.95

MURDER IS RELATIVE by Karen Saum. 256 pp. The first
Brigid Donovan mystery.   ISBN 0-941483-70-3   8.95

PRIORITIES by Lynda Lyons 288 pp. Science fiction with
a twist.   ISBN 0-941483-66-5   8.95

THEME FOR DIVERSE INSTRUMENTS by Jane Rule. 208
pp. Powerful romantic lesbian stories. ISBN 0-941483-63-0   8.95

LESBIAN QUERIES by Hertz & Ertman. 112 pp. The questions
you were too embarrassed to ask.   ISBN 0-941483-67-3   8.95

CLUB 12 by Amanda Kyle Williams. 288 pp. Espionage thriller
featuring a lesbian agent!   ISBN 0-941483-64-9   8.95

DEATH DOWN UNDER by Claire McNab. 240 pp. 3rd Det.
Insp. Carol Ashton mystery.   ISBN 0-941483-39-8   9.95

MONTANA FEATHERS by Penny Hayes. 256 pp. Vivian and
Elizabeth find love in frontier Montana. ISBN 0-941483-61-4   8.95

CHESAPEAKE PROJECT by Phyllis Horn. 304 pp. Jessie &
Meredith in perilous adventure.   ISBN 0-941483-58-4   8.95

LIFESTYLES by Jackie Calhoun. 224 pp. Contemporary Lesbian
lives and loves.   ISBN 0-941483-57-6   9.95

VIRAGO by Karen Marie Christa Minns. 208 pp. Darsen has
chosen Ginny.   ISBN 0-941483-56-8   8.95

WILDERNESS TREK by Dorothy Tell. 192 pp. Six women on
vacation learning "new" skills.   ISBN 0-941483-60-6   8.95

MURDER BY THE BOOK by Pat Welch. 256 pp. A Helen
Black Mystery. First in a series.   ISBN 0-941483-59-2   9.95

BERRIGAN by Vicki P. McConnell. 176 pp. Youthful Lesbian —
romantic, idealistic Berrigan.   ISBN 0-941483-55-X   8.95

LESBIANS IN GERMANY by Lillian Faderman & B. Eriksson.
128 pp. Fiction, poetry, essays.   ISBN 0-941483-62-2   8.95

THERE'S SOMETHING I'VE BEEN MEANING TO TELL
YOU Ed. by Loralee MacPike. 288 pp. Gay men and lesbians
coming out to their children.   ISBN 0-941483-44-4   9.95

LIFTING BELLY by Gertrude Stein. Ed. by Rebecca Mark. 104
pp. Erotic poetry.   ISBN 0-941483-51-7   8.95

ROSE PENSKI by Roz Perry. 192 pp. Adult lovers in a long-term
relationship.   ISBN 0-941483-37-1   8.95

AFTER THE FIRE by Jane Rule. 256 pp. Warm, human novel
by this incomparable author.   ISBN 0-941483-45-2   8.95

SUE SLATE, PRIVATE EYE by Lee Lynch. 176 pp. The gay
folk of Peacock Alley are *all cats*.   ISBN 0-941483-52-5   8.95

CHRIS by Randy Salem. 224 pp. Golden oldie. Handsome Chris
and her adventures.   ISBN 0-941483-42-8   8.95

THREE WOMEN by March Hastings. 232 pp. Golden oldie. A
triangle among wealthy sophisticates.   ISBN 0-941483-43-6   8.95

RICE AND BEANS by Valeria Taylor. 232 pp. Love and
romance on poverty row.   ISBN 0-941483-41-X   8.95

PLEASURES by Robbi Sommers. 204 pp. Unprecedented
eroticism.   ISBN 0-941483-49-5   8.95

EDGEWISE by Camarin Grae. 372 pp. Spellbinding
adventure.   ISBN 0-941483-19-3   9.95

FATAL REUNION by Claire McNab. 224 pp. 2nd Det. Inspec.
Carol Ashton mystery.   ISBN 0-941483-40-1   8.95

KEEP TO ME STRANGER by Sarah Aldridge. 372 pp. Romance
set in a department store dynasty.   ISBN 0-941483-38-X   9.95

HEARTSCAPE by Sue Gambill. 204 pp. American lesbian in
Portugal.   ISBN 0-941483-33-9   8.95

IN THE BLOOD by Lauren Wright Douglas. 252 pp. Lesbian
science fiction adventure fantasy   ISBN 0-941483-22-3   8.95

THE BEE'S KISS by Shirley Verel. 216 pp. Delicate, delicious
romance.   ISBN 0-941483-36-3   8.95

RAGING MOTHER MOUNTAIN by Pat Emmerson. 264 pp.
Furosa Firechild's adventures in Wonderland. ISBN 0-941483-35-5   8.95

IN EVERY PORT by Karin Kallmaker. 228 pp. Jessica's sexy,
adventuresome travels.   ISBN 0-941483-37-7   9.95

OF LOVE AND GLORY by Evelyn Kennedy. 192 pp. Exciting
WWII romance.   ISBN 0-941483-32-0   8.95

CLICKING STONES by Nancy Tyler Glenn. 288 pp. Love
transcending time.   ISBN 0-941483-31-2   9.95

SURVIVING SISTERS by Gail Pass. 252 pp. Powerful love
story.   ISBN 0-941483-16-9   8.95

SOUTH OF THE LINE by Catherine Ennis. 216 pp. Civil War
adventure.   ISBN 0-941483-29-0   8.95

WOMAN PLUS WOMAN by Dolores Klaich. 300 pp. Supurb
Lesbian overview.   ISBN 0-941483-28-2   9.95

SLOW DANCING AT MISS POLLY'S by Sheila Ortiz Taylor.
96 pp. Lesbian Poetry   ISBN 0-941483-30-4   7.95

DOUBLE DAUGHTER by Vicki P. McConnell. 216 pp. A Nyla
Wade Mystery, third in the series.   ISBN 0-941483-26-6   8.95

HEAVY GILT by Delores Klaich. 192 pp. Lesbian detective/
disappearing homophobes/upper class gay society.
                                          ISBN 0-941483-25-8   8.95

THE FINER GRAIN by Denise Ohio. 216 pp. Brilliant young
college lesbian novel.   ISBN 0-941483-11-8   8.95

THE AMAZON TRAIL by Lee Lynch. 216 pp. Life, travel & lore
of famous lesbian author.   ISBN 0-941483-27-4   8.95

HIGH CONTRAST by Jessie Lattimore. 264 pp. Women of the
Crystal Palace.   ISBN 0-941483-17-7   8.95

OCTOBER OBSESSION by Meredith More. Josie's rich, secret
Lesbian life.   ISBN 0-941483-18-5   8.95

LESBIAN CROSSROADS by Ruth Baetz. 276 pp. Contemporary
Lesbian lives.   ISBN 0-941483-21-5   9.95

BEFORE STONEWALL: THE MAKING OF A GAY AND
LESBIAN COMMUNITY by Andrea Weiss & Greta Schiller.
96 pp., 25 illus.   ISBN 0-941483-20-7   7.95

WE WALK THE BACK OF THE TIGER by Patricia A. Murphy.
192 pp. Romantic Lesbian novel/beginning women's movement.
                                          ISBN 0-941483-13-4   8.95

SUNDAY'S CHILD by Joyce Bright. 216 pp. Lesbian athletics, at
last the novel about sports.   ISBN 0-941483-12-6   8.95

OSTEN'S BAY by Zenobia N. Vole. 204 pp. Sizzling adventure
romance set on Bonaire.   ISBN 0-941483-15-0   8.95

LESSONS IN MURDER by Claire McNab. 216 pp. 1st Det. Inspec.
Carol Ashton mystery — erotic tension!.   ISBN 0-941483-14-2   8.95

YELLOWTHROAT by Penny Hayes. 240 pp. Margarita, bandit,
kidnaps Julia.   ISBN 0-941483-10-X   8.95

SAPPHISTRY: THE BOOK OF LESBIAN SEXUALITY by
Pat Califia. 3d edition, revised. 208 pp. ISBN 0-941483-24-X   10.95

CHERISHED LOVE by Evelyn Kennedy. 192 pp. Erotic
Lesbian love story.   ISBN 0-941483-08-8   9.95

LAST SEPTEMBER by Helen R. Hull. 208 pp. Six stories & a
glorious novella.   ISBN 0-941483-09-6   8.95

THE SECRET IN THE BIRD by Camarin Grae. 312 pp. Striking,
psychological suspense novel.   ISBN 0-941483-05-3   8.95

TO THE LIGHTNING by Catherine Ennis. 208 pp. Romantic
Lesbian 'Robinson Crusoe' adventure.   ISBN 0-941483-06-1   8.95

THE OTHER SIDE OF VENUS by Shirley Verel. 224 pp.
Luminous, romantic love story.   ISBN 0-941483-07-X   8.95

DREAMS AND SWORDS by Katherine V. Forrest. 192 pp.
Romantic, erotic, imaginative stories.   ISBN 0-941483-03-7   8.95

MEMORY BOARD by Jane Rule. 336 pp. Memorable novel
about an aging Lesbian couple.   ISBN 0-941483-02-9   9.95

THE ALWAYS ANONYMOUS BEAST by Lauren Wright
Douglas. 224 pp. A Caitlin Reece mystery. First in a series.
                                           ISBN 0-941483-04-5   8.95

SEARCHING FOR SPRING by Patricia A. Murphy. 224 pp.
Novel about the recovery of love.   ISBN 0-941483-00-2   8.95

DUSTY'S QUEEN OF HEARTS DINER by Lee Lynch. 240 pp.
Romantic blue-collar novel.   ISBN 0-941483-01-0   8.95

PARENTS MATTER by Ann Muller. 240 pp. Parents'
relationships with Lesbian daughters and gay sons.
                                           ISBN 0-930044-91-6   9.95

THE PEARLS by Shelley Smith. 176 pp. Passion and fun in
the Caribbean sun.   ISBN 0-930044-93-2   7.95

MAGDALENA by Sarah Aldridge. 352 pp. Epic Lesbian novel
set on three continents.   ISBN 0-930044-99-1   8.95

THE BLACK AND WHITE OF IT by Ann Allen Shockley.
144 pp. Short stories.   ISBN 0-930044-96-7   7.95

SAY JESUS AND COME TO ME by Ann Allen Shockley. 288
pp. Contemporary romance.   ISBN 0-930044-98-3   8.95

LOVING HER by Ann Allen Shockley. 192 pp. Romantic love
story.   ISBN 0-930044-97-5   7.95

MURDER AT THE NIGHTWOOD BAR by Katherine V.
Forrest. 240 pp. A Kate Delafield mystery. Second in a series.
                                           ISBN 0-930044-92-4   9.95

These are just a few of the many Naiad Press titles — we are the oldest and
largest lesbian/feminist publishing company in the world. Please request a
complete catalog. We offer personal service; we encourage and welcome direct
mail orders from individuals who have limited access to bookstores carrying
our publications.